THE PSYCHIC TOUCH

Memory Guild Book 2

WARD PARKER

Mad Mangrove Media

ISBN: 978-1-7345511-7-4

CONTENTS

AUTHOR'S NOTE

The city of San Marcos, the setting of this tale, was inspired by St. Augustine, Florida, a truly unique and magical place. However, I wanted lots of *supernatural* magic! And monsters, too! So I created the alternate world of San Marcos. While some details and historical references may seem familiar, San Marcos is entirely fictional, as are all the characters, names, and places described herein.

CHAPTER 1

DIVE RIGHT INTO THE STORY

I once read you can survive a three-story fall if you land in just the right way.

Dennis Simpson of Athens, Georgia, did not. He landed head-first on the ancient cobblestone street outside my inn. He hit the stones so hard, I heard it from my bedroom where I was still awake. If I had been asleep, the screams of his wife from their open third-story window would have awakened me quite effectively.

I rushed outside in my T-shirt and sweatpants. I live in a guest house attached to the courtyard behind my inn. When I exited the gate in the thick stone wall, spectators were already gathering around the fallen body. It was before midnight, but most of them were probably tourists, except for a neighbor I recognized who was walking his small dog.

Is it horrible that one of my first thoughts was the negative publicity my inn would get from this death? Don't answer that. I know it was horrible.

I called 911 on my cellphone as I approached the body. The

operator said they'd already been contacted, and paramedics were on the way. One glance at the crumpled body on the cobblestones, and the spreading lake of blood, told me it was too late for paramedics. I shuddered at the sight.

From this vantage point, I saw the open window and noted it was room 303.

Great. The haunted room. Just what I needed for bad publicity and urban legends in the making. Mrs. Simpson, in a flimsy nightgown, stuck her head out the window and shrieked. I needed to get up there fast to comfort her. And keep her from bringing attention to the open window of my inn. Already, the onlookers were staring up at her. I thought I heard someone say "haunted."

I raced inside and up the stairs to the third floor. The stairs were faster than the small, rickety elevator. I went around the open landing and knocked delicately on the door of 303.

There was no response, other than muffled sobbing.

The door of 304 opened.

"Has something happened?" asked the elderly German tourist.

"There's been an accident, but it's being taken care of," I said, hoping he'd close his door. He did, but slowly.

The Esperanza Inn had eleven guest rooms, one of which was a true suite, though two others were large enough that I misleadingly called them suites. Only four of the rooms were occupied. The inn had only recently opened under my proprietorship, so thirty-six percent occupancy wasn't terrible, but this was high tourist season, so I should have been doing better.

Which returned me to the topic at hand: One of my four booked rooms had a dead guest. The name of my inn would be all over the local news, more exposure than it received from the paltry advertising I could afford.

And before you knock me for being cold-hearted, I felt terrible about the tragedy. However, I'm a control freak, especially when it comes to my emotions. To avoid being overcome by them, I always put myself into action mode. After all, I was in charge at my inn and needed to act like it.

I knocked on the door again.

"Mrs. Simpson?" I called in a voice sounding more soothing than I felt. "Please open the door. It's Darla. The owner."

No response except for muffled sobbing. I wish I had my pass key.

"Mrs. Simpson, the police will be here soon."

Finally, the bolt clicked, and the door opened. Monique Simpson was petite like me, but she had curly auburn hair. Her face was pale and streaked with tears.

"I'm so sorry," I said. "Are you okay?"

"Of course I'm not okay."

I agree, it was a stupid question. I'm not experienced with comforting guests whose husband just took a header from my third-story window.

"Is he dead?" she asked timidly.

We both knew the answer.

"The paramedics will be here any moment," I said.

"He looks dead from here. This is our twentieth anniversary. How could he die like this?"

"How did it happen?" I asked. It was none of my business, and I was not a cop. But sometimes, I don't have much of a filter.

The window, from which Mr. Simpson had made his final exit, was wide open. The decades-old curtains fluttered in the breeze. A half-empty bottle of single-malt Scotch sat on a table beside two chairs in the sitting area. An empty bottle of champagne rested in an ice bucket. My theory was Mr. Simpson was sitting on the windowsill and, in his drunken state, lost his balance and fell.

An alternate theory was that the couple had quarreled, and he took his own life. That was a bit more of a stretch.

The possibility that Monique had pushed him out the window came in a distant third in probability. She was small and her husband had been a fairly large guy. She wouldn't have been able to pick him up and toss him out. But maybe if you considered him being drunk, the window being open, and him standing beside it or sitting on the sill, and give her a running start, maybe, just maybe, she could have launched into him and pushed him out.

So which was the winning answer?

"He didn't jump," Monique said. "He never would have done that. It was the ghost. The ghost threw him out."

YOU MIGHT THINK IT WAS RIDICULOUS TO SUGGEST A GHOST threw one's husband from the window of your accommodations. But this was the Esperanza Inn, formerly the Hidalgo Inn, and the Simpsons were staying in Room 303. This room was infamous for being haunted. The previous owner of the inn, who himself had died in mysterious circumstances years before I bought it, hyped the haunting in his brochure.

The ancient City of San Marcos, Florida, was thronged with ghosts from over the centuries, and there were no fewer than four companies giving ghost tours for tourists. Having a bona fide ghost was actually a bonus feature that helped the inn stand out from the scores of quaint inns and bed-and-breakfasts.

The ghost was said to have been of a young newlywed who was killed by her jealous husband in the eighteen hundreds.

How? By pushing her from the window, of course. The cobblestones of the street below were truly unforgiving.

I believed in the ghost story. With a bit of the paranormal in my blood, I sensed her presence early on after buying the property. I have even caught brief glimpses of her.

The Simpsons stayed in this very room for part of their honeymoon twenty years ago and insisted on doing so for their anniversary. The ghost was part of the allure, though they told me when checking in that they didn't see her during their previous stay.

I also had experienced the murderous husband's thoughts. I have the ability of psychometry to pick up the traces of psychic energy people leave upon an object they've touched and read their thoughts and memories. This energy can linger for decades, centuries even. The first time I opened the door to this room, I was overcome by the extreme emotions the husband had left on the doorknob when he, too, turned it. He was full of rage and jealousy over the idea that his new wife had been unfaithful. I experienced those thoughts and emotions as if I were inside his head, as if I were him for a brief moment. It was horrifying.

And the funny thing was, a murderous ghost wasn't the only supernatural resident I inherited with this place. I had other ghosts and occult entities here, including some I hadn't yet encountered directly.

Oh, and don't forget the living gargoyle who slept beneath the fireplace mantel in the front room downstairs. And there was also the vampire who lived in a crawlspace behind the kitchen, whose presence I had to endure because he insisted he was the rightful owner of the place.

Neither of these supernatural fellows would ever end up in my brochure, I can promise you.

"Are you absolutely sure it was the ghost?" I asked.

"Yes. I saw her. She pushed Dennis from the window."

"I've never heard of the ghost having a physical effect—moving things or pushing people," I said. "Those who have experienced her only saw a brief spectral image."

"She was whispering in my husband's ear. That's what he said. She was telling him to kill himself. He complained of it all evening long and was getting very agitated. I thought he was having a mental breakdown or something. But then I saw her. She wore a Victorian-era dress, a long thing that touched the floor. She appeared behind him when he stood by the open window and pushed him out. Then she smiled at me while I screamed, until she faded away and disappeared."

I didn't believe it. Just because I believed in ghosts didn't mean I was gullible.

"But she's not that kind of ghost."

"I watched my husband's murder, and you're defending the ghost?"

"No, of course not, I'm sorry."

I had no attachment to the ghost. But there are different sorts of hauntings, and this ghost was only a visual specter. Certainly not the kind who could push a living human from a window. She didn't even move small objects or make rattling noises like some ghosts.

On the other hand, after being thrown to her death by her husband, her ghost doing the same to a man had a certain poetic justice to it. Or am I being evil to think that?

Back in the world of the living, I gave Monique a quick hug.

"Again, I'm so, so sorry," I said. "Please stay here at no charge for as long as you need."

She nodded. But started crying again. I guided her to a chair in the sitting area and moved the bottle of Scotch to a less-visible place behind a lamp.

The ceiling filled with red and yellow lights projected from emergency vehicles below. The front desk bell made my phone buzz. It was probably the police. I rushed downstairs.

"Ah, Ms. Chesswick. We have to stop meeting up at death scenes."

It was Detective Michael Samson. You might say there'd been some chemistry between us in the past, but it was complicated by his seeming lack of respect for my psychometry. I had chalked it up to him being a hard-nosed cop who didn't believe in the paranormal. But then, I found out he had supernatural blood in him.

In short, Detective Samson was a werewolf. Though he took great pains to keep it secret, especially from his coworkers.

I never revealed to him I was telepathic. Which gave me a distinct advantage whenever he got flirty or feigned indifference.

"Hello, detective. For the fiftieth time, you can call me Darla."

"And you can call me Mike."

He smiled, and it was sincere. Samson wasn't handsome like a model, but handsome enough, his features weathered by middle-age and the Florida sun. He had a cleft chin, a nose slightly hooked, and a full head of dark curly hair half turned to gray. And he was in good shape, in a natural, not gym-rat way. The San Marcos Police polo shirt he wore was tight enough to show some musculature, but also the slight suggestion in his belly that more than one beer had been consumed in this man's life.

"Which room did the victim fall from?" he asked, all business. "I assume the wife is still in there?"

"Three-oh-three. And yes, she's there. Want me to bring you up there?"

"Thanks, but I have to wait for another detective. I can't interview a woman without another person there."

"How about me?" I asked.

He laughed. "That won't be necessary."

"She told me a ghost did it," I said. "Can you believe that?" I hoped he couldn't.

"Great," he said, shaking his head sadly. "What a way to end my shift."

A woman entered the lobby wearing the police department polo shirt. She was tall. Well, taller than me, but many people were. She was artificially blonde, perky breasted, and strangely familiar. Then it hit me.

I had bumped into Samson at a touristy seafood restaurant not long ago. He had been on a date. With this woman. Wasn't intra-departmental dating frowned upon at the police department? Apparently not.

Samson couldn't restrain a grin when he saw Ms. Perky enter my inn.

"Cynthia, this is the inn's owner, Darla Chesswick. Darla, meet Detective Lepore."

"Sorry to meet you," I said. "I mean, sorry to meet you under these circumstances."

Detective Perky gave Samson a questioning look.

"The victim's wife is in three-oh-three," he said.

"I'll show you up," I offered.

"No thank you," Detective Perky said. "It's best if you wait down here."

I watched them climb the staircase. I didn't let them know there was a small elevator around the corner. Too small for coworkers of the opposite sex to share.

When I realized the feeling I was experiencing was jealousy, I was ashamed. I'd been on this earth a hair longer than fifty years, been married twice, and had no excuse for a petty emotion like jealousy.

I was surprised I felt it at all.

You see, I recently stumbled upon the possibility—no, actually it was a farfetched theory—that my second husband didn't walk out on me one night without a word after all. That was what all evidence pointed to him doing. I left the room where he was reading and returned an hour later to find him gone. He didn't leave a note or take a change of clothing. He just vanished. For the past year, I assumed he just slipped out the back, Jack. He took the simple route out of marriage.

Then, I faced the possibility that he didn't run away on purpose. He . . . wait, this is going to sound insane. You'll think I'm creating a desperate conspiracy theory to spare my ego. But I'll explain in due time.

I believe Cory might have accidentally slipped into an alternate plane of reality, a different dimension. And then, he couldn't return.

Please don't laugh.

In the Esperanza Inn, a door to the attic has appeared now and then, usually in different locations. Soon afterwards, it would disappear, leaving no trace it was ever there.

And the thing is, the building doesn't have an attic.

Lest you assume the doors were figments of my imagination, I actually opened one once, went through it, and climbed partially up a staircase. But I experienced strange, uncomfortable sensations, so I exited into the hallway. Not long afterwards, the door disappeared.

If I had gone up those stairs to the attic that didn't exist, I probably would have disappeared, too.

My cousin, Missy, is a witch. I don't mean her personality; I mean, she practices magic. She has lots of paranormal in her blood and said she passed through similar portals before to an alternate plane of existence. It's called the In Between. She warned me against going there because it was dangerous.

I read Cory's memory from just before he disappeared, in which he was about to check out a closet that didn't exist. What if he went to the In Between and can't return to this world?

Yeah, maybe it was a desperate conspiracy theory. But it gave me something to think about other than Samson's curly locks. It would be like my husband was captured in war, while I believed he was dead and started dating again.

Missy dampened my hopes. She said if Cory had gone to the In Between, it wasn't likely he survived.

It was best if I stopped thinking about him and my bizarre theory. And not to think about men at all. My inn had only just opened and hadn't proved yet that it would survive. I still had lots of renovations to do. And I had many other things demanding my attention, from my kooky witch mother to my adult daughter who still couldn't stand on her own two feet.

And I had my duties as a member of the Memory Guild. I'll explain about that later.

In short, I had endless things to keep my focus away from a husband who up and left me.

But the truth was, if that attic door ever showed up again, I would probably go through it.

Samson and Perky returned downstairs about an hour and a half later. I should probably refer to his colleague by her real name. What was it, Detective Leper?

Samson looked tired. Both their expressions were stoic.

"Is she still blaming the ghost?" I asked.

"You know I can't divulge what was said in an interview,"

Samson said. "Mrs. Simpson will need to stay here for a little while longer, until we ascertain no charges will be filed. I hope you have a room for her."

Of course I had a room. I was only at thirty-six percent occupancy. But now I worried about my offer for her to stay gratis. What if she was charged with a crime, bonded out, and needed a place to live during a long trial? Surely, she wouldn't expect my offer to extend to that. Right?

"We'll be on our way now," Samson said. "We're sorry for the tragedy on your property."

"Thank you. Goodnight, Detective Samson, Detective Leper."

"Lepore," Ms. Perky corrected.

"My apologies," I said.

GIVE UP THE GHOST

I knocked lightly on the door to 303.

"Mrs. Simpson? It's Darla checking on you."

The door opened. Monique was pale and haggard, with the shine of recent tears on her cheeks.

"Were the detectives polite?" I asked.

"Polite enough. Until I mentioned the ghost. They were skeptical, to say the least. They asked many questions about Dennis' mental state. I suppose suicide is a more believable cause of death than a ghost."

My thoughts exactly. The last thing I needed were rumors spreading that I had a ghost in my inn that kills guests. Most old buildings that have held many people get reputations of being haunted. Maybe a few people avoid the buildings for that reason, while countless others are intrigued. Few, like the Simpsons, would want to stay in the very room said to be haunted by the ghost, but others are charmed by the notion that the residence or hotel has spectral occupants.

But no one would enter a building knowing they could be

killed by an evil spirit. It sounds heartless, I know, but I'd rather the truth be that Dennis took his own life. Maybe, the ghost made an appearance before he jumped, but I hoped it would become clear that the ghost wasn't to blame. Having encountered her myself, I didn't think she was.

"Dennis didn't seem depressed at all," Monique said. "In all our years together, he never mentioned suicide. I just can't—I can't believe he killed himself. So, I suppose, in the eyes of the police, that leaves me as the main suspect. As if I would want to bring to myself the pain I feel now."

"Would you like coffee or tea?" I asked. "Or a little breakfast?"

The empty champagne bottle and depleted bottle of Scotch indicated some food in her stomach would be a good idea.

Monique nodded. I smiled and led her downstairs to the kitchen.

The Esperanza Inn served a full breakfast daily for my guests, as well as freshly baked scones and finger sandwiches for afternoon tea. I always had cookies available in the common rooms. The kitchen was also available to caterers who booked my downstairs rooms for events, should any such caterers actually want to book them. I anxiously awaited that day to come.

I made coffee, toast, bacon, and scrambled eggs. I nibbled on toast while she scarfed down the meal. I talked about the renovations I planned for the kitchen, such as new cabinets and up-to-date appliances. I wanted to keep as much historical detail as possible. The cabinets I would replace came from the 1970s, so they were no loss. But the floors were ceramic tile at least a century old, so they would stay. The enormous butcher-block island was even older. The deep copper sink had to stay, too.

I had already done some work, such as remove cabinets and drywall that had covered a window to the courtyard. I had no idea why someone would have covered it. The fact was the kitchen showed signs of having evolved quite a bit over the centuries. In fact, the original building, built in the early seventeen hundreds, didn't even have a kitchen. In those days, the cooking was done in an outbuilding for fire safety. I wasn't sure what this room had been originally, but it made a great kitchen with the heavy oak beams on the ceiling and the small fireplace, next to which sat the table where we ate.

It was so cozy, I frequently forgot about what was behind one of two refrigerators: a door to a crawlspace where the vampire slept. And, speaking of the dead, the topic which we were trying to avoid came up again.

"Is it possible the ghost encouraged Dennis to kill himself?" Monique asked.

I had a hard time believing this. I had only glimpsed her as a fleeting apparition. And no one who reported seeing the ghost, in articles I'd read about the inn before I owned it, ever mentioned her communicating. The Simpsons were the first guests since I opened to have seen her.

"I suppose," I said guardedly. "No one has reported hearing her before. Did you?"

"No. But she came into close contact with Dennis, her face near his ear. Perhaps, she was whispering to him and guiding him to the window, rather than pushing him."

"Perhaps. Look, I'm sure the detectives asked you this, but are you absolutely certain he didn't fall from the window by accident? A little too much champagne or Scotch? Was he sitting on the windowsill?"

She could have used this explanation and avoided the lengthy interrogation and putting herself under suspicion.

"The detectives said he landed face-first," Monique said.

"And that a witness saw him fall. He didn't fall backwards like someone sitting on the windowsill with his legs in the room."

"Oh." It sounded like she had tried that scenario with the cops and failed. The interrogation might have been more contentious than I had assumed.

Now was the time to use my telepathy invasively. Don't get the idea that I'm a master telepath. I'm not. Usually the phenomenon occurs when someone's thoughts enter my mind unbidden. Often, it's the thoughts they would least want someone else to hear, like disparagements, secret desires, or the need to find a toilet.

However, when a person is comfortable with me, and I'm free of distractions, I can concentrate really hard on them. Sometimes, I can infiltrate their thoughts and hear some. That's what I attempted to do to Monique. I hoped my intense stare didn't give me away.

I easily picked up anxiety that the police suspected her of murdering her husband and a lot of thought fragments about the interrogation.

But when I probed deeper, trying to pick up on her memories of what really happened, I hit a brick wall. I wasn't surprised. People don't enjoy reliving traumatic situations. They repress these memories. But they always come bubbling up, eventually.

I had another paranormal tool in my tool belt: my newly discovered psychometric abilities.

"Do you believe in psychics and things like that?" I asked.

"Well, I believe in ghosts, obviously. I believe there are authentic psychics out there, but most of the ones who do it for money are scam artists.

"Right. What would you say if I told you I can touch an

object and sometimes experience the thoughts or memories of people who had handled that object?"

"I'd be a little dubious," she said.

"Of course you would. Now, it doesn't work all the time and with every object. Often, it's really powerful emotions, or recurring memories, that stick to an object. Like that coffee cup you're holding. It might have a bit of your psychic energy, or it might have someone else's from years ago. I didn't pick up on anything when I took it from the cabinet, but I wasn't in the right frame of mind. Do you mind if I touch it now?"

She pulled the cup closer to her, a look of concern on her face. Then, after a long pause, she pushed it toward me.

"Give it a try," she said.

I took the handle in one hand and wrapped my other around the cup. No thoughts filled my head. During the short time that I'd had this ability, which appeared with the earliest signs of menopause, I'd held a few objects that practically screamed at me. Others were silent or filled with indecipherable gibberish. I was learning techniques of controlling my ability that I learned from Laurel, the other psychometrist in the Memory Guild.

I cleared my mind of everything, except the feeling of the cup's porcelain in my hands. I opened my senses. I drew upon my inner spirit. Then, I waited.

Soon, a clutter of whispering came into my head from many voices. The set of coffee cups had already been in the cabinet when I bought the inn. I didn't know how old they were or how many hands had held them over the years. I kept my distance above the cacophony of whispers and searched for the most recent thoughts.

Finally, I found something very recent and plunged into the memory. I looked up at Monique.

"So you were thinking I'm making this up?" I asked.

A big grin filled her face.

"You did it! You proved me wrong."

"The reason I bring this up, is maybe we can learn your husband's thoughts right before the end. So we'll know if he wanted to take his life."

"Oh, that would be too painful right now." A tear inched across her cheekbone.

"Of course. I understand,"

The truth was whatever I learned from reading one of Dennis' possessions would be irrelevant to the police. Samson had told me in the past that he was not totally against using psychics to help solve child abductions or close cold cases. But I knew my perception of the mental state of Dennis would not prove he killed himself or show that his wife did it. It might help nip this ghost nonsense in the bud, though.

I tried reading Monique's thoughts again. Once more, I was blocked. I could tell she was very intelligent.

It occurred to me that perhaps she was playing a game. Blaming Dennis' death on a ghost was so outlandishly illogical to most people that Monique looked like a kook. Who else would use that as an alibi? It made it more difficult to portray her as a cold, calculating murderer. Suicide seemed more likely, and people would assume she was too soft-headed to accept the fact her husband killed himself.

My theory made me much more suspicious of Monique Simpson.

If she brought murder to my inn, she deserved to pay the price. I resolved to find out if that was the case, not just to absolve my resident ghost, but because justice demanded it.

Monique's eyelids drooped. She looked like she was about to pass out from exhaustion, despite the two cups of coffee she had downed.

"Let me get you to bed," I said. "It's nearly three o'clock. You've been through way too much tonight."

"Thank you for being with me. You're too kind."

"Not at all. Come along."

I offered her a hand and helped her up from her chair. She was completely deflated. What a traumatic night it had been for her.

"My head," she said, placing her palm against her temple. "Do you have any aspirin or ibuprofen?"

"Of course."

I found a bottle of generic pain relievers in my what-not drawer and shook out a couple of tablets into her hand. I filled a tall glass with ice and water and handed it to her. She took the pills and returned the glass to me. I refilled it.

"Take this with you to bed. Let's go."

I led her to the small elevator, and we rode it to the third floor. She seemed ready to collapse at any moment. All the grief, adrenaline, and shock had left her but a husk of the chipper personality she had been when they checked in the previous day. I put my arm around her as we walked down the hall, lit only by wall sconces that lengthened the shadows and added drama to the historical oil paintings spaced regularly along the walls.

This time, I had remembered my pass key. No electronic locks for my historic inn, only brass keys attached to wooden discs with each room number engraved. My pass key had a larger disc that was blank. I opened the door and helped her to her bed. I placed the water glass on the bedside table and turned on the lamp, then switched off the other lights in the room.

"Let me get this junk out of your sight," I said, gathering the empty glasses that reeked of Scotch and the steel bucket with melted ice and the empty bottle of champagne.

"Try to get some sleep," I said as I left the room. "I'll tell the housekeeper not to disturb you."

"Thank you," she said.

"Good night." I closed the door.

I took the elevator back down, but instead of leaving the dirty whiskey glasses and champagne flutes in the kitchen sink, I carried them with the empty bottle to my cottage.

I planned on reading them, to see what memories might cling to the glass. Perhaps there were memories of what preceded Dennis Simpson's death.

That would wait, though, until later in the morning. I needed to be fully rested to get a decent reading.

I left the glassware on my tiny dining room table. The two-bedroom cottage used to hold vacationing families, but now it held the humble innkeeper, who stumbled to the bed where she had been four hours ago when all the trouble began.

Cervantes, the black cat who had shown up one day to adopt me, was still curled up on the end of the bed, oblivious to all the tumult outside. He opened one eye to look at me as I turned off the light and crawled into bed beside him.

My nerves were still taut, but I fell asleep quickly.

It wasn't a heavy sleep. The creaking of my front door caused my eyes to snap open and my heart to race.

Cervantes dove beneath the bed, brave guard-cat that he was.

Glassware clinked. I jumped out of bed and hurried from my bedroom.

Monique stood in my living-dining room beside the table

where her glassware sat. She wore the bathrobe that came with her room. She stepped away from the table when she saw me.

"Monique?"

"I'm so sorry to bother you," she said meekly. "But do you mind if I change rooms? It's so oppressive in mine, I can't sleep."

"I understand," I said. After all, her husband had fallen to his death from that room.

"I feel the presence of the ghost. She's hostile toward me. I feel she wants to harm me like Dennis."

Oh boy, here we go again.

"Do you have another room available?"

"Unfortunately, I have many rooms available," I said. "Let's get you set up."

I slipped on my sandals and led the way across the courtyard to the front desk.

"I tried calling, but there was no one here at the desk. But that's okay in a small inn. I didn't want to call the emergency number."

I grabbed the key for 201.

"We'll put you on a different floor, give you some distance from the other room." I grabbed the key. "Let's get what you need for tonight, and I'll move your bags from 303 later in the day."

"I'm sorry I'm such a bother," she said as we headed for the stairs.

We gathered her nightgown, a change of clothes, and her personal care items, then brought them to 201. We said goodnight as she climbed into bed and placed the drinking glass on the bedside table. I turned off the light as if I were putting a child to bed.

When I went downstairs, I wrote a note for the housekeeper, since I was definitely going to be late showing up, and returned to my cottage. I glanced at the glassware on my table and wondered if Monique had actually intended to take it away so I couldn't read it. Why hadn't she knocked? Why did she just let herself in? But, frankly, I was too tired to really care. For the third time, I went to bed.

AND FOR THE THIRD TIME, I WAS PULLED OUT OF BED AGAINST my will. Someone was banging on my door. My watch said it was noon. Boy, had I overslept.

It was Julie, my housekeeper. She was hysterical.

"The guest you moved to 201. . ." Julie was hyperventilating.

"What? What's wrong?"

"She's dead."

CHAPTER 3

A TIDY MURDER

"Did you call nine-one-one?" I asked Julie as we hurried up the stairs to 201.

"I thought it proper to inform you first."

"What if she's not dead and needs emergency care?"

"Oh, she's dead all right."

Julie opened the door with her passkey, and I hesitantly stepped inside.

Julie was right. Monique Simpson was dead, no doubt about it.

The recent widow lay on her back where I had last seen her, her eyes open and her mouth gaping in a quizzical expression. The water glass I had given her was now empty.

You could also use the word "empty" to describe Monique; the contents of her abdomen were missing entirely. It looked like the empty shell of a blue crab.

Despite the gruesomeness of the corpse, there was very little blood on the sheets. And the bed wasn't even messed up. The whole thing had been done with perfect neatness.

"Where are her, you know?" I asked in a whisper.

"I don't know. I didn't look for them."

A fly flew into the bathroom. Now I knew where to look.

Room 201 had a beautiful antique clawfoot bathtub. This is where the rest of Mrs. Simpson lay.

Will you forgive me for being relieved that the organs were placed here, instead of all over the bedroom, so the cleaning bill would be less extreme? No, you probably won't forgive me. But I should add that only a few droplets of blood ran from the bed to the bathroom. How was that possible?

I noticed two bloody footprints pointing from the bathroom to the bedroom. The odd thing was they were barefoot feet.

After Julie saw the bathtub, she got sick in the toilet. I went into the hallway, called 911, then plopped down onto the floor, my back against the wall. The trauma of what had happened, and what I'd seen, was threatening to shut me down.

I hadn't trusted Mrs. Simpson and suspected she pushed her husband from the window. But no one deserved to die like that. I hoped she had lost consciousness too quickly for her to suffer much.

The young couple from Georgia, the only other guests on this floor, walked down the hall on their way outside to see the sights in San Marcos.

"Are you okay?" the wife asked me.

"Couldn't be better," I said. "Have a wonderful day."

After they went downstairs, I jumped to my feet and returned to the room just as Julie was fleeing it. I retrieved the water glass from beside the bed before the police showed up. Now, I had an entire collection of glassware to read for memories. That was the only thing I could think to do to help my situation. I had a newly opened bed-and-breakfast inn operating now at only twenty-seven percent occupancy.

And I had two dead guests in less than twelve hours.

It was probably too late for my inn to avoid being nicknamed "the Death Inn." But I needed to make sure I didn't lose my other guests in the same fashion. Was there a serial killer stalking the place? Or was it true that my resident ghost was a murderer?

I brought Monique's water glass to my cottage, sensing her psychic residue on the glass, but not having the time or concentration to read her memories now. I needed to devise a strategy. Soon, the police would be here, giving me hours of distractions.

I paced back and forth in my tiny living room, trying to think. Okay, the serial killer theory didn't add up. Dennis' death was self-inflicted or caused by his wife. Or by a ghost. Monique's death looked like it was enacted by a psychopath. A very tidy psychopath. But how did this person get into her room?

The killer-ghost scenario was becoming more likely. Along with my bankruptcy.

The only good news was the police and medical examiner arrived at a good time. It was when all of my guests were away from the inn, taking selfies at the fort that once guarded the city, or buying kettle corn in the tourist district. There weren't any reporters here yet, and if I was really lucky, there wouldn't be.

Samson probably had the day off after working a late shift the night before. Instead, Ms. Perky took my statement as I sat behind the mahogany table that serves as the front desk.

"Welcome back, Detective Leper," I said.

"Lepore. Le-*pore*."

"Sorry about that."

She knew I didn't like her. I didn't try to read her mind, but her thoughts drifted into my head that I was jealous of her body and her face like Wonder Woman's. I didn't care.

"Did Mrs. Simpson request to move to another room," the Leper asked.

"Yeah. In fact, she came into my cottage without knocking while I was asleep. She said she was having nightmares in 303. I could understand that."

"Did you see the Simpsons interacting with anyone after they arrived at your inn?"

"No. They didn't come to tea that afternoon. And I served wine and cheese in the early evening so guests could mingle, but they didn't attend. I didn't see if they went out for dinner, though I assume they did."

"Who has pass keys to the rooms?"

"I have one. I keep it with me at all times, or locked up in my cottage. The other one, along with the duplicate room keys, is kept locked in this drawer here." I pointed to the shallow drawer above my lap.

"The housekeeper has a key to that drawer?"

"No. Just me, or whoever is working the front desk. But since the inn opened, it's just been me. So I give Julie, Julie Fodder, and my other housekeeper, the pass key when they come in each day."

I remembered something that made my heart skip a beat.

"Um, except today, I slept late because of all that happened last night. I left a note for Julie with the pass key behind the coffeepot in the kitchen."

The leper scribbled furiously on her notepad.

"Who cooked breakfast today?"

"I did. I left it on the warming trays and went back to bed."

"What about handymen or other workers? Do they have access to the key?"

"No. I unlock rooms for them, when needed."

She wrote some more.

"So, I didn't see any signs of forced entry on Room 201," I said. "Is that why you're asking me about the pass key?"

"Just a routine question, ma'am."

No, it wasn't. I picked up a few thought fragments from her. Julie and I were the most obvious suspects she needed to scratch off her list.

"What about a knife?" I asked.

"What?"

"Did you find a murder weapon?"

"The crime scene techs are gathering evidence. That's all I'm allowed to say."

I really burrowed into her mind this time. She was remembering an antique dagger with a jeweled handle she found under the bed in 201.

Interesting. The knife definitely wasn't mine. Was it Monique's? That would mean she was gutted by her own weapon. But by whom? I've never heard of a ghost attacking a person with a weapon, only of poltergeists tossing bric-à-brac at people.

Detective Perky Leper asked me more questions that sounded perfunctory, while my attention wandered to ghosts and daggers. Finally, she left. But the crime scene techs stayed for hours after the body was taken away in a zippered bag. They were going to put yellow crime-scene tape across the door until I talked them into using only a sticker covering the keyhole. That would be bad enough, if any guest noticed it.

Perky Leper had searched 303 again, as did the crime-scene techs, though they didn't seal it off. Julie and I would have to pack the Simpson's belongings and send them to any next-of-kin we could find. That is, if Julie ever came back. I truly hoped she would, but couldn't blame her if she didn't.

She had applied for the housekeeping position right before I opened. She was a hard worker and cleaned all the rooms herself. I also had a part-time housekeeper who worked on the weekends and could back Julie up if I ever had a full house. Which I haven't. Julie was middle-aged and had once been an educator before falling on hard times. I thought she was the greatest and hoped what she had seen today wouldn't make her quit.

When my guests began streaming back in from their touristy adventures, I set out wine and cheese on a table in the foyer and retreated to my cottage. After I scarfed a microwaved frozen dinner, eaten standing up in the kitchen, I sat down at my little dining table. It was time to attempt reading the glassware I had taken. If this didn't work, there were the possessions that Monique had left in 303. I could try those, too.

The champagne bottle had a little bit of energy clinging to it. I wrapped my hands around it, but no memories jumped out at me. I would have to coax them out.

There were thoughts from Dennis. Sentimentality about their anniversary. Fragments from a corny toast he made. That was about it.

Next, I held a champagne flute, the one without lipstick smears. I wanted to continue his chain of thought. Again, nothing very strong on this glass. Hopes for spontaneous sex. Satisfaction after the sex. Musings about missing their reservations for dinner with no regrets.

Then there was a hint of dark thoughts. About what I couldn't tell. I was intrigued and wanted to continue his train of thought.

I picked up the tumbler that was free of lipstick. And right away—

—I can't believe it! She promised me she had quit that stupid squad. She promised! And here we are on our twentieth anniversary and she's going to do a hit! She lied to me! All that nonsense about

wanting to see the ghost and reliving our honeymoon—it was all lies. I can't believe it! We're staying in this stupid inn just so she can kill the owner? On our anniversary! I feel so betrayed. Now she's denying it again. I want to—

—I came out of my trance as his thoughts ended abruptly. Maybe this was when he dropped the glass and spilled the Scotch.

I was trembling. Getting caught up in a strong connection like that and reliving someone's powerful emotions was as draining as if I experienced them myself. Well, in a way I had.

The other reason for my trembling was what the man was thinking. If I perceived it correctly, Monique was some sort of hired killer who came here to murder me.

I couldn't grasp it. It was too crazy. Why in the world would she want to kill me? I never knew these people. Though I'm no angel, I can't think of anyone I've wronged badly enough to be killed for it. I just run small inns. And not very successfully.

The only reason I could think of was my membership in the Memory Guild of San Marcos. We're a benign group, for sure. But I helped take down a power-hungry madman and his sorceress girlfriend. The man, Norman Knobble, "The Carpet King," was dead. His girlfriend was behind bars, or so I thought. Did she arrange for my murder?

I shook my head at the insanity of it all.

Now it was time to read the glasses that Monique was using, in case her thoughts and emotions were preserved there. If I didn't learn what I needed to know, I'd go through her other belongings. At least the ones she hadn't brought with her when she moved to the now-sealed Room 201.

I dreaded experiencing what was in the mind of this woman, who wasn't who I thought she was.

Oh, wait, I thought. It's getting late. I should return to the inn to put the wine away and dispose of the leftover cheese and crackers before a rat or cockroaches do it for me.

I know, I was procrastinating. Can you blame me?

There were a lot of cheeses and crackers left because I had so few guests. I covered the tray with plastic wrap and stuck it in one of the kitchen fridges. I corked up the remaining wines and sherries and put them away. Except for the bottle of Rioja Reserva. That baby was coming back to the cottage with me.

Once in my living room, I poured a glass of wine and took a deep sip. Then, I sat down at the table again and prepared to work my wonders.

THE CHAMPAGNE FLUTE WITH THE SMUDGE OF GARNET lipstick refused to give up Monique's thoughts. Instead, a low humming filled my head. It was an uncomfortable pitch that made me feel edgy, like a knife scraped on a plate. I'd never experienced this before when reading an object. Her mind must have been filled with evil intent while she sipped champagne in Room 303, sitting on the bed or in a reading chair, listening to her husband utter romantic banalities he hoped would seduce her.

Amid the humming, I picked up thoughts of killing. They were technical images: how to conceal a handgun in the pocket of her cardigan sweater. How close to the target to get before removing the gun. Where on the rear of the target's skull to aim. It was like a mental rehearsal of a task to be carried out.

Then I saw a brief glimpse of a face. It was mine. The face of the assassin's target.

I returned the flute to the table and removed my hand. I didn't enjoy seeing myself as prey to be killed. Would you?

I would have to read the tumbler next. The husband's had

been full of raw emotion as the drinking session graduated to the hard stuff, drunkenness, inflamed passions, and Monique revealing the truth about her mission. Unlike the lightweight champagne flutes, his glass held a great deal more psychic energy. It has been my observation, and the other psychometrist of the Guild agreed with me, that denser, more substantial materials hold memories better.

Now, it was time to test that theory with Monique's glass.

The glass felt good in my hand, its solid weight, its decorative etchings. I had splurged buying such expensive drink-ware for the rooms, especially since some would be broken or stolen. But guests appreciate touches of luxury.

The scent of single-malt Scotch rose to my nostrils from the dried residue at the bottom. I turned the glass, allowing the light above me to glitter from the—

—I wish he would stop pouting. He knew very well that I was an assassin when he married me, because he was a client! I took out his mistress when she threatened to tell his first wife about their affair. He had no qualms at all about my work back then. Oh, Lord, there he goes again about betrayal and all that nonsense. He's upset that I'm mixing business with pleasure, that I'm not one hundred percent focused on him this weekend. He's such a baby. If it weren't for me, we'd be living in a trailer somewhere with his salesman's salary. Salesman at a second-rate jeweler . . . Lord, will he please shut up for a moment? We shouldn't have kept drinking on an empty stomach. I've got this miserable headache, and he's put me in such a mood . . . oh, now he's bringing up Rachel, just to throw her in my face. He promised me he'd never mention her name again . . . what? Is he serious? He can't be. He's saying that just to rile me up . . . why, you little cheating jerk!

(Flash of light)

I need a drink . . . need to erase the memory of hitting him with both hands, pushing him, screaming, get away from me! Go! Go! Pushing . . . oh, no, no. What have I done? What have I—

—I dropped the glass. It bounced off the table and landed on the floor. The glass was fine, but my cheap table now had a nick.

My hands were shaking. I couldn't get the image out of my mind of her hands against Dennis' shoulder blades, pushing him until he tripped and fell toward the open window. His head glanced against the bottom of the sash, and then he plunged, flailing at the air.

It was horrifying. And I was overcome with guilt, as if I were the one who killed him. I couldn't slow down my breathing. I took a long swallow of Rioja, silkily running down my throat.

Well, that reading answered a lot of questions. Dennis didn't kill himself, and my resident ghost didn't do it either. His annoyed wife did it.

The same woman who intended to kill me, too.

She didn't strike me as an assassin. She was petite and cute, though her eyes were awfully cold, now that I thought about it. Or at least cold toward me, her target. I was surprised she was strong enough to push her husband out of the window. She also seemed genuinely heartbroken that her husband had died.

The tall glass I had given her with drinking water sat on the table, waiting for me to touch it. I had to do it. I needed to know if it held Monique's last thoughts.

I picked it up. Nothing hit me at first. I wrapped both hands around it where traces of her fingerprints had been left. I cleared my mind and waited.

Grief and anguish came over me, rolled over me, smothered me. These feelings were more intense than when I had held the Scotch glass. Part of me resisted, but I—

—shouldn't have done it. It threw me off my game. Passion should

never come into play when you kill. And I didn't even want to kill him. And look at me—crying all night like a delicate little housewife. When I went to Chesswick's cottage, I totally blew it. I got distracted seeing our drink ware on her table, knowing she could read our thoughts from it. I should have gone straight to her bedroom and completed my mission. But she woke up, and I was not in the state of mind to fight her and take her down. No way. So I allowed her to send me to bed like a little daughter who had nightmares . . . but I did have nightmares. Of the ghost getting revenge on me for blaming her . . . oh, Lord, I don't think I can complete this mission. I'm not on my A Game. My concentration is shot. I'll ask for someone else to do it . . . I hope this water doesn't make me wake up having to pee . . . what was that noise? Don't tell me the ghost followed me to this room—

—And that was that. Not her last thought before dying, but the last one recorded as a memory, held by this glass, to be read only by people like me. I set down the glass.

So this left me with two overwhelming desires. One was to find out what had killed Monique. Was it my resident ghost, who was still not off the hook? Or did her assassin's squad get to her unbelievably quickly?

And my other desire was to find out if they were still coming after me, and, if so, why.

CHAPTER 4

SAGE INSIGHTS

With all the drama of the past twenty-four hours, I hadn't had the opportunity to speak with Archibald. And he wasn't always available for speaking, because Archibald was a gargoyle. He could be the most lively, loquacious guy of the party, but most of the time, he was just an impish stone figure that helped support the Medieval mantel above the fireplace in the front room downstairs. In other words, gargoyles spend most of their time sleeping like a rock, though they're always aware of what's going on around them.

Supernatural gargoyles like Archibald aren't permanently anchored to the masonry where you normally see them. They can transport themselves (how, I do not know) and appear affixed to just about any stone surface sturdy enough to support them. Perhaps to wood, too, though I've never seen this. And certainly not to drywall.

"Archibald? Do you have a moment?"

I stood before the stone facade imported from England by one of the inn's nineteenth-century owners. There were three other, non-sentient, gargoyles supporting the mantel with Archibald. The impish, demonic-looking heads were about the size of cantaloupes and rested on little hands with claws.

"Archibald, I don't mean to bother you, but I really need your advice."

Archibald, too, was a member of the Memory Guild. He was a stone-reader who delved into the secret histories of the rock and masonry that had built this city since the fifteen hundreds.

"Rise and shine, Archie," I said, placing my hands on his cold, hard head.

The stone vibrated and then moved. I yanked my hands away.

"Never call me Archie."

"Sorry. I needed you to wake up."

"Annoyed isn't a pleasant state in which to wake up."

"*Archibald*, what do you know about an assassin squad or guild?"

"I've never heard of one. There isn't one in San Marcos as far as I know. Although, I suppose they'd be very secretive about it if there were."

"Well, please be extra vigilant. I've learned that an assassin was ordered to kill me. I'm not worried about her anymore, because she was killed. But someone else might come instead."

"Good heavens, it has been busy here. I certainly will be vigilant. Is there anything else you can tell me?"

"That's all I know for now. But I have another question: Do you know anything about the ghost in Room 303?"

"She was thrown from the window by a jealous husband in 1889. Her name is Helga, I believe. From what I've observed, she's merely an apparition that appears to humans from time to time."

"Has she ever hurt someone?"

"As I said, she only exists as a visual manifestation. She doesn't have the power to harm anyone."

"Are there any ghosts here who have harmed anyone?"

"No, not ghosts. Well, there was George, who had a very unpleasant personality. He threatened guests in a scary voice and slammed doors and such. But I don't believe he ever actually hurt anyone. He hasn't been around for at least a hundred years, so I don't know what happened to him."

"The reason I'm asking is the assassin who was killed, the one who was going to kill me, killed her husband. And then, she was killed."

"Egad, it was a festival of killing last night!"

"I have my doubts, though, that a human could have pulled off the killing of the assassin so quietly and neatly."

"Ah, I detected something evil upstairs, but it didn't stay here long. That's all I know."

"How can I learn more?" I asked.

"Sage can help you better than I with what's going on in the spiritual realm. Gloria can summon her for you."

Gloria Salter was, in many ways, your stereotypical psychic. She had a small storefront in Old City, a block off of the main tourist drag, where she read palms and Tarot Cards. Of course, her studio had one of those crystal balls. She was also a medium and would hold seances for clients willing to pay the hefty fee.

But Gloria wasn't a scam artist; she was the real deal. That's why she'd been invited to join the Memory Guild. She didn't just tell you what the future held in store for you; she could see the entire past of your current life and any lives you may have led before it. With its mission to increase humankind's knowledge of history, as well as preserve its accuracy, the Memory Guild needed members with paranormal abilities like Gloria's.

Also, as a medium, Gloria was one of the summoners of Sage,

a ghost who didn't believe she was a ghost. Sage was the Guild's liaison to the spiritual world and thus was very valuable to our mission. I hoped Archibald was correct, and Sage could help me solve my ghost conundrum.

"No, it doesn't have to be night and we don't have to hold hands," Gloria said as she sipped a cup of tea in my living room. The large windows faced the courtyard with its fountain and small garden. Gloria was a petite older woman with short, silver hair that glowed in the sunlight from the windows behind her.

"How do you summon Sage?" I asked.

"I don't summon her. I invite her to join me. Isn't that right, Sage?"

"Yes," a female voice said, though I didn't see where it came from.

"Let Darla see you, dear."

"I'm right here. Been here all along."

Sage materialized on the piano bench. The piano made a wonderful focal point for the room, but I couldn't play it, and I didn't know when the last time was it had been tuned.

Sage launched into "Feelin' Alright" by Joe Cocker. She was quite good, with a bluesy style. Unfortunately, the piano was not quite in tune.

I explained to the two of them, the living and the ghost, what had happened in the inn two nights ago.

"The guest blamed a ghost for her husband's fall, which was actually caused by her. Then she was murdered, and I'm guessing it was by something supernatural. Is there any way you can help me know for sure?"

"I would have to ask around," Sage said, stopping her performance. She had long, gray hair tied in a ponytail. Her apparition did, I mean. Sage departed from this world shortly after Woodstock. In fact, possibly because of something she ingested at Woodstock.

She faded away and the piano bench was empty.

"Did she leave?" I asked.

"She'll be back. She knows several other sentient spirits like herself. It's like the gossip club of the spirit world. Hopefully, one of them knows something."

Sage materialized on the sofa next to Gloria.

"You're back!" I said. "That was fast."

"Time is meaningless on the other side," Sage said. "I have your answer. There's been some talk, and it's not good. A demon has passed through here recently. A major demon, extremely powerful. Not the kind of visitor we want in San Marcos."

I'm pretty sure my mouth dropped open. Until fairly recently, I didn't know for sure that ghosts existed. I had no idea that gargoyles could come alive. And I didn't even believe in vampires. The only supernatural stuff I knew about was witchcraft, because my mother was a witch, more of a hobbyist, and my cousin Missy was one, too, but pretty powerful.

It's been a lot to absorb, all this supernatural craziness.

"Thank you, Sage, and Gloria. Please warn me if you hear of this demon coming back."

"We will, dear," Gloria said.

"And I don't want to alarm you, but the Guild should know I have a price on my head."

"What?" said both visitors, alive and dead, at the same time.

"I read some objects handled by my dead guests, and the wife is a member of some sort of squad, and she was sent here to kill me. Though Archibald said he's never heard of such an entity."

"Neither have I. But I'll ask to convene a meeting of the Memory Guild right away so we can protect you," Gloria said. "In fact, I'll stay here to look out for you."

"Thanks, but please no. I can't put you in danger, too. And you're not a bodyguard."

"I'll stay with you," Sage said. I couldn't see where she was at the moment. "I can't stop an assassin, but I can give you plenty of warning."

I didn't have to worry about her getting killed, after all. It was a little too late for that.

"Thanks. I would appreciate that. Do you see death in my future, Gloria?"

She took my hand and stared at me intently, long enough to make me uncomfortable.

"I see only murkiness," she said. "Your fate is undetermined at the moment."

It wasn't what I wanted to hear. But I thanked my fellow Guild members profusely, and Gloria returned to her psychic parlor. Sage disappeared to do whatever ghosts do. And I went on to what I did every day: be in perpetual servitude to a high-maintenance inn that was nearly three hundred years old and to the few guests I had, who knew they could be more demanding because I needed them so badly.

Julie, fortunately, had shown up for work. She seemed okay. I asked her if she was.

"I try not to think about it," she said while she put fresh towels into her cart. "I averted my eyes as much as I could when I was in 201, so I'm hoping the images in my mind will fade away."

"Keeping your mind focused on work will help," I said.

"It's not as if making beds requires that much mental effort."

"Um, yeah," I mumbled. I kept forgetting that she had been a professor or something. "Well, let me know if I can help."

"What about you?" She fixed me with her intense gray eyes. She had a large forehead and brown hair cut short, but her face from the eyes down was narrow. That made her brain case look unnaturally large.

"Me? I've been too busy for it to truly sink in."

It occurred to me that trying to brush the horrible deaths aside could be bad for my mental health. I wasn't a combat veteran or a first responder with experience in dealing with the traumatic deaths of others. I was just an innkeeper.

"You bring up a good point," I said. "I think I'll talk to someone about it."

"Good," Julie said. "That's what I'm going to do."

I allowed her to get back to her job, which involved, sadly, only two rooms to clean and the common areas to vacuum. I set about baking scones, halving the recipe in case no one showed up for tea.

And no one did. My guests were obviously too busy seeing the sights of San Marcos to return to the inn. I set out a small portion of scones in the foyer, put some in a bag for Julie, and decided to bring the remaining portion to Gloria to thank her for coming to see me.

Her psychic parlor was much classier than what you're envisioning. No "psychic" neon sign, no crystal ball in the window, no bored woman sitting on a chair waiting for the next mark to come in. Instead, the window was framed by hunter-green drapes, and the signage was subtle gold-leaf lettering that announced, "Gloria Salter, Psychic Consultations." A tiny bell rang when I opened the door.

"Ah, Darla! What a pleasure to see you twice in one day."

She sat at a desk in the rear of the room. By the way, there *was* a crystal ball atop her desk. The front of the room was taken up by a seating area with two love seats facing each other with a coffee table in between. A deck of Tarot cards sat on the table.

"Is Sage still guarding the inn?" Gloria asked.

"As far as I know. She doesn't always make her presence known."

"I'm sure she's there. She's very responsible for a ghost. She's not like those flighty spirits."

"She's very transparent about her intentions."

"I see what you did there."

"Gloria, can I stop in sometime this week to speak with you? Not to foretell my future, but to let me air out my feelings about the deaths I just experienced."

"Of course you can."

"I've never been to a psychologist before, but I figure you're more perceptive than any shrink."

"That's a wonderful idea. It would be good for you. I have the rest of the afternoon free."

"Oh, I should get back to the inn. Too much to do. I'll call you later in the week to set up a time."

We said our goodbyes, and I left her shop. The weather was cooling down nicely as the evening approached. Salt from the bay spiced the air among the scent of grilled fish from a nearby bistro.

I waited for a pedicab to pass before I crossed the one-lane street on the corner of Gloria's block. Screeching tires made me look back at her shop.

An old SUV was parked in front. I gasped when I saw the driver exit the car. He was a man in black military tactical gear with two rifles strapped across his chest. A black balaclava covered his head and face.

He went into Gloria's shop.

Without thinking, I raced after him.

I was only a few doors away, but my sprint seemed to take forever. Finally, I burst through the door with the tiny tinkling bell, expecting to hear a fusillade of gunshots.

Instead, the assailant was struggling with his gear. He attempted to aim a semi-automatic rifle at Gloria, who was taking cover as best she could behind her desk.

The rifle's strap was entangled with the strap of the man's second rifle, and with a pistol holster and other gear hanging from his body armor. The more he struggled, the more tangled up he got.

A shot rang out, and I flinched. The man whimpered, and I realized he had shot himself in the foot. He tried to wrestle his gun barrel upwards to a horizontal position, but it snagged in his baggy tactical trousers.

He abandoned this idea and reached for his pistol. But in all his gyrations, the holster was twisted and pushed toward his back, and the handle was encircled by the strap of his other rifle.

I almost felt pity for the man.

I walked past him to Gloria's desk, grabbed her crystal ball in both hands, and slammed it on the man's head. His foot slipped in the blood pooling around his wounded foot, and he went down. He landed on the floor with a clatter of steel and plastic. I worried one of his grenades was going to explode, but it didn't. The man was out cold.

"This crystal ball is darn heavy," I said to Gloria.

THE PARAMEDICS WHEELED AWAY THE COMMANDO handcuffed to the gurney with a police officer in tow. The cuter of the two paramedics assured me the head injury I had caused would not be fatal and, at the most, had caused a concussion. I hoped he wasn't just trying to make me feel better.

"Was he one of the assassins coming after you?" Gloria asked.

"No one knew I'd be at your shop," I said. "He was there to kill you. I'm not the only one who is targeted. I think some assassin squad is coming after all the members of the Memory Guild. And their assassins aren't very good."

CHAPTER 5

HOLDING A GRUDGE

I wasn't yet a full, tenured member of the Memory Guild, only a provisional member on probation. I could not simply text the members and say, "hey, buds, let's meet up." They would summon me. Which meant waiting for Archibald to get me.

How does a gargoyle "get" you? As I said before, the little stony headed guy traveled around, somehow, supernaturally. And he always showed up when I least expected him.

The morning after the attempt on Gloria's life, I weeded the planters in the courtyard. I was on my knees in the mulch among the African Lilies and Purple Coneflowers, when I heard Archibald's voice.

"There's been another assassination attempt," he said in his gravelly voice with the crisp English accent.

I looked up to see him above me, mounted to the massive coquina wall that separated the courtyard from the street.

"Oh, no," I said. "Is everyone all right?"

"Yes, except for the would-be assassin. The perpetrator came after Dr. Noordlun."

Dr. Noordlun was the director of the Memory Guild and the chair of the history department at San Marcos College.

"Dr. Noordlun was driving across the Segovia Street Bridge when the assassin rammed his car and tried to force it off the bridge and into the river," Archibald continued. "Dr. Noordlun out-maneuvered the other car, which lost control and slammed into the rear of the truck in front of them. The assassin hadn't noticed the drawbridge was going up and traffic was stopping. Well, the truck he hit was carrying a load of portable loos—what do you Americans call them? Porta-Potties? The toilets fell off the truck. Apparently, they hadn't been emptied of their contents, which poured in a big tidal wave of sewage onto and into the assassin's car. He tried to flee, slipped in the poo-slime, and fell off the bridge."

"Wow," I said. "Did he drown?"

"No, he was fortunate enough to land on a boat that had just passed under the bridge. But unfortunate enough that it was a commercial shrimping boat, and he landed in the open hold among all the netted shrimp."

"Was he arrested?" I asked.

"We don't know. He wasn't when the police interviewed Dr. Noordlun."

"The assassins are oh for three," I said.

"They remain a severe threat. The Guild is meeting about it."

"When?"

"Now."

I suddenly wasn't in the courtyard anymore. I was floating in darkness, surrounded by stars. You see, the Guild usually meets virtually, and by virtual, I do not mean via computer video conference. I mean via astral travel. Our spirit selves get together for the meeting. And getting there was a real trip.

After hanging, seemingly motionless, in the starry darkness, I suddenly dropped. Even though I wasn't there physically, my stomach shot up into my throat. Or at least, I imagined the sensation of it. It wasn't pleasant.

Soon, what I was falling toward came into view: a planet covered in molten lava. This was not a place I wanted to visit.

But soon the lava disappeared as the planet morphed into one covered by an endless ocean. I barreled toward it and plunged beneath the surface. I sank deeper and deeper until I was forced to take a breath. Like in a dream, I found I could breathe.

A strange, primitive, fishlike creature swam by. Its mouth was lined with needle-like teeth. Fortunately, it didn't notice me.

I touched bottom. Then, I realized the bottom was rising, an undersea mountain growing from the depths. I rode it as it broke the surface of the sea, and more fishlike creatures wiggled from the water onto the land toward me. Before they could reach me, I was flying into the air.

A flock of pterodactyls flew past me.

Are we there yet? I wanted to ask.

We've been there for quite some time, Archibald said in my head. *History is a constant journey. We must never forget that.*

I flew past the emerging land and was above an ocean again that stretched from horizon to horizon.

Tiny objects caught my attention below. I swooped lower to get a better look. They were three wooden sailing vessels, emblazoned with the coat-of-arms of Spain.

Then the passage of time sped up as I flew through a jungle trail and passed a column of Spanish troops wearing steel cuirasses. Not far head of them, Aztec warriors were on the retreat. Then I was above a peninsula—Florida, at last! But this Florida was untouched by modern humans. It teemed with birds, deer, alligators, panthers. It was covered with forest, savannas, and wetlands sprinkled with white birds. There were no high-ways, shopping malls, or sprawling suburbs of cookie-cutter homes.

My heart ached at seeing my beloved home in its early inno-cence. But then, on a bay in the Northeastern part of the state, a city rose. A giant fort was slowly built from blocks of coquina limestone. San Marcos came into being. It grew and spread, but before it reached the contemporary era, I flew away against my will.

And found myself standing in a stone room with a domed ceiling that felt as if it belonged in a castle. The lights on the walls were glowing orbs. And standing before me were the other nine members of the Memory Guild:

Dr. Noordlun with his white goatee; Diego, the 500-year-old African-American vampire; Laurel, the other psychometrist in her wheelchair; burly, bearded James, the metal-speaker; wispy Summer, the wood-speaker; and elderly Diana, the astral witch. Then there was Gloria, Sage, and, of course, Archibald, attached to the wall above us.

"Sorry, am I late?" I asked.

"We all arrived at the same time," Archibald said.

"You're all looking so serious," I said.

"This is a serious matter," Dr. Noordlun said. "We're under attack."

"Not very effectively," I said.

The director frowned at me. "Do not be confident their incompetence will always be the case."

"Who would want to kill us all?" I asked. My manic, overly talkative side had taken over, probably because I was nervous. I'm told this side of me can be charming or annoying, depending upon the audience. In this case, I saw a lot of frowns.

"As our mission is to protect the truth of history, our greatest enemy is the Father of Lies," Dr. Noordlun said.

"You mean Satan?"

"Not literally. The Bible gave Satan that name, but the Father of Lies actually exists in other manifestations."

"I don't understand."

"You won't, until you've been in the Guild for a while," Diego said. "The Father of Lies can appear as a human, or demon, or an illness of the mind spreading throughout the populace. He is a threat to us, not simply because his lies fight the truth, but because we are the repository of all memory, in case humankind's means of archiving history are ever destroyed. The Father of Lies would love that more than anything."

I understood even less now, but I wisely kept my mouth shut.

"We must begin our search for suspects by reviewing those we've thwarted who might seek vengeance," Dr. Noordlun said.

An image of a large-breasted blonde appeared floating in the air, a hologram of sorts. The woman was Esmerelda, whom my first ex-husband thought he was dating. At the same time, she was involved with the Carpet King and his murderous attempt to obtain an enchanted coin that would give him tyrannical power over people if he achieved his political ambitions.

"This woman was thwarted by our newest member, Darla. But she's currently serving time in the county jail. There seems to be no evidence that she has access to the funds required to hire assassins."

"And I think she would only want to kill me," I said, "not the entire Guild."

"We don't know that for sure," Archibald said.

Esmeralda disappeared, replaced by the hologram of a man with a thick head of hair and a bowtie. I recognized him as a former local news anchor who disappeared from the airwaves.

"You all know this odious fellow, Lance Mewling," Dr. Noordlun said. "On his Sunday talk show, he was a constant source of misinformation, conspiracy theories, and outright lies. We politely petitioned the station to rein him in. They didn't. We organized a boycott of his show's sponsors, but that wasn't effective either. When he began embracing Holocaust denial, we had to take extreme measures."

"Extreme measures?" I asked, concerned.

"Nothing violent or illegal, I assure you," Archibald said. "Mewling was fired and discredited."

"When the moment is right, we will teach you our methods," Dr. Noordlun said. "In the meantime, focus on our most important technique: ferreting out the historical truth."

Another hologram appeared, a muscular, bald guy with a short white beard.

"Jules Monsignor," the director said. "Treasure diver. He plundered the wreck of a newly discovered Spanish galleon that was under the state's protection as an archeological site. He excavated the gold illegally, and his equipment and methods destroyed the wreck, making it impossible for archeologists to identify. We were able to identify it, and we tracked down Mr. Monsignor, reporting him to the authorities."

"Wow," I said. "How did you do that?"

"Laurel did psychometric readings of some tools accidentally left behind by Monsignor and discovered whose they were. And Summer communicated with a section of wood from the hull the archeologists gave us. She found the ship's name, which was matched with records from Spanish archives."

More holograms appeared in rapid succession.

"The people I have mentioned are from recent Guild assignments, and they have the resources and ability to attempt retribution against us. But we thwart enemies of history every day—grave desecrators, museum thieves, vandals, spreaders of disinformation. So, we have many enemies."

"Humans who are alive today," Archibald said. "But we have also righted wrongs that were done in the past. Who knows if the dead seek vengeance?"

No one spoke for a while.

"What is really bothering me," I said, "is who killed the assassin who was assigned to kill me? And why?"

Diego the vampire said, "The squad she belonged to killed a member who failed in her mission. It sends a message to its other members not to fail."

"The fact that the three attempts against us have been utter failures doesn't mean we should let down our guard," Dr. Noordlun said.

"Their squad has awfully lax standards for admitting members," said Gloria.

"Keep an eye on the news to see if the last two 'assassins,'" Diego said, using air quotes, "are killed. The one who attacked Gloria is probably out of the hospital and in jail right now. I don't know if the one who rammed Dr. Noordlun's car was arrested."

I remembered an alert from the local newspaper I received on my phone earlier, before Archibald told me of the attack and whisked me off to this virtual meeting.

"Um," I said, raising my hand. "I think the fellow from the bridge is already dead."

"What makes you say that?" Dr. Noordlun asked.

"I read a news alert that someone was accidentally fed through a shrimp processing machine at the city wharf."

"One less assassin to worry about," Archibald said.

"It should be clear to all of us that our task goes beyond finding who commissioned the hits against us," Dr. Noordlun said. "We must also stop this squad, even if they seem to be stopping themselves without our help. There is no registered Assassins' Guild or similar organization in San Marcos."

"How can we stop them?" Diana, the astral witch, asked.

"All the supernatural guilds of the city must band together and drive the rogues from our city," Dr. Noordlun said.

"Easier said than done," Archibald muttered. "The guilds of this city never get along."

"An uncharted guild that isn't paying into the general fund? Oh, that would surely inspire united opposition," Dr. Noordlun said. "But first, we must take action against the party that commissioned the assassins. Ms. Chesswick!"

"Um, yes?" Why was he calling on me?

"You're still provisional, so you get the first assignment. Before we move on to the other suspects, find out if this black-magic woman you fought is whom we're seeking."

"Yes, sir. But, um, I'm a psychometrist. How am I supposed to investigate a woman in jail?"

"You have your specialty, Ms. Chesswick, but all of us have learned to push ourselves beyond our natural abilities and gifts. The Memory Guild has a very broad mission. And we all must expand our comfort zones to accomplish it. Am I correct that you also are telepathic?"

"Yes, Dr. Noordlun. It's spotty, though."

What I wanted to say was, Esmerelda is behind bars, and you're not paying me. This isn't a real job. I have an inn to run.

But I didn't say that. Because I knew I was part of a unique group of individuals with a mission I could believe in.

And I was honored to be one of them.

But that didn't make this assignment any easier.

CHAPTER 6

GOSSIP GIRL

Esmerelda was in the county jail, a twenty-minute ride from town. She was awaiting trial on charges of assault, battery, kidnapping, and arson. It sounded devastating, but it would be an uphill battle for prosecutors to convict her.

Esmerelda was a witch who practiced black magic. That wasn't a crime in our criminal code. She had summoned a demon that killed a man in this very jail, and she had confessed to it on video. But how do you convince a jury of that?

It would be a lot easier to prove she took part in the kidnapping of yours truly, when she, her evil boyfriend, and a couple of thugs captured me and kept me at a motel waiting for me to pass a magic coin I had swallowed (long story). There was also evidence that she had violently assaulted my cousin Missy and me, and burned a bedroom in my inn. The problem was, she had committed the above crimes with black magic. I didn't know how the prosecutors were going to explain that.

Esmerelda still looked thin and pretty behind the plexiglass window at the jail visitation room, though she'd cut her blonde hair short. The jail jumpsuit didn't look half bad on her.

I hated her. Mostly because of what she had done to me. But also because she had dated my ex-husband Number One while cheating on him with the evil carpet-seller.

Based on her expression, she didn't like me much either.

"What could you possibly want?" she asked.

"You don't believe I'm here just to say hello?"

"Get to the point."

"To be honest, I'm here to see how much you hate me," I said. "And you're making that readily apparent."

"You didn't need to come all the way here to learn that."

"Okay, I'll be direct. Someone hired assassins to come after me and my friends. I think it was you."

She laughed. "I wish."

"That's why I'm here."

"Because of you, Norman Knobble is dead. He would have been the great ruthless dictator we Americans deserve."

"It was his own fault he died. He sought forbidden power."

"He could have had it if you and your witch cousin hadn't disrupted my spell to protect him."

"So now, you're having me killed," I said.

"I can't. I don't have the money. Norman left me a lot in his will, but his wife and family are contesting it. I have all these legal fees. And my event planning business is obviously ruined. I'm flat broke."

"So you got someone else to pay the assassins."

She shook her head. "Nope. If you're trying to invent an additional charge to throw against me, good luck. The cops won't find any evidence at all."

"Have you heard of an assassin squad or guild?" I asked.

"Nope. I don't care much about guilds after I got harassed by the Magic Guild for practicing black magic. As far as I'm concerned, even the Rotary Club is too much trouble."

"Okay. Well, if you were to hire an assassin, where would you go?"

"Don't play tricks with me, Chesswick. You act like you're a dizzy-headed chick, but I know you're just trying to entrap me. I have nothing to do with what you're talking about. I think we're done here."

She was right. I wasn't going to get anything else out of her. But I would not rule her out yet, either.

Samson finally called me back while I drove home.

"Took you a while to return my call," I said. "I guess you figured your friend, Leper, got everything pertinent from me."

"Lepore. Her name is Lepore."

"Whatever. Look, I have more information about the murder of my female guest. The source of my information prevented me from telling Le-*pore*."

"Ah, some psychic stuff?"

"That's right."

Samson had always acted begrudgingly open to the truth of my psychic abilities, while still skeptical of the entire subject. Once I learned he was a werewolf, the balance of power changed between us. We both knew secrets about each other. In fact, he would lose his career if his secret got out. So the detective had to take me seriously.

"I read some objects touched by the Simpsons," I said. "It was clear that Monique pushed Dennis from the window, mostly out of anger."

"I see."

"They were having a spat because what he thought was a romantic getaway was actually a business trip for her. She was an assassin, and she was there to kill me."

"Wow. Are you serious?"

"Absolutely."

"So, all this talk about a ghost was nonsense?"

"The ghost in three-oh-three did not kill anyone. But I wouldn't be surprised if something supernatural killed Monique. Did Leper—I mean, Lepore—brief you on the condition of the body?"

"She did. But she believes a human did it, of course. And guess which humans are at the top of her list of suspects? You and your housekeeper."

"Oh. Were prints found on the dagger?"

"I'm not supposed to say this, but I will: only the victim's prints were found. But the killer could have been wearing gloves."

"Whatever. Are you really telling me I'm a suspect?"

"It's just the beginning of the investigation. I wouldn't worry about it. But I also wouldn't leave town if I were you."

How comforting.

When I returned to the inn, I did some internet searching about the other most-recent people who might have a grudge against the Guild. Dr. Noordlun hadn't said who would be assigned to investigate them, but I was curious.

There wasn't much of interest about the treasure diver. Monsignor was famous for his finds and even had a museum displaying some of the most famous (and impossible to sell) artifacts. The only negative mentions were about the destructive incident that made him a target of the Guild.

Monsignor was fined over a million dollars. But he didn't

receive any criminal charges. He was not ruined in any sense. I didn't see a motive for hiring assassins.

The other guy, Lance Mewling, had his broadcast career ruined, but he still lived on in the dankest fringes of the internet. And he appeared to be doing even better than before, financially. He was born and raised in San Marcos, and I went to school with him. But if anyone knew the skinny about him, it was my old friend, Jen.

Jen and I were friends since grade school. We were especially close in high school. I went to the local college, and she went off to the University of Florida, but she was living in town after graduation and warned me not to marry Buddy, my first husband. She remembered all the trouble he'd gotten into in high school. Of course, I didn't listen to her. And, of course, I regretted it not long after having my daughter.

Jen and I were close again, now that I was back in San Marcos, after a six-year stint running a B&B in Key West until Husband Number Two disappeared. Jen and I were the ladies who lunched and brunched and had boozy dinners. She was also the realtor who handled my purchase of the inn.

Today, after I served breakfast to my guests at the inn, I met Jen for coffee in a small courtyard cafe in Old Town. When she arrived, we air-kissed and talked about her husband and kids, as well as my crazy mom and vexing daughter.

Then I got down to business.

"How well do you know Lance Mewling?" I asked.

"Not too well. He was two grades ahead of us."

She was being modest. If there was dirt, she'd know it.

"It's rather sad that he turned out to be the most famous person to come out of our high school, at least in our generation," she said. "And he turned into a total nut-bag."

"Yeah, I remember him as a journalism geek. Editor of the school newspaper and all that."

"But there were hints, even back then, of the kind of extremism he would get into."

I gazed at Jen's face across the small table. Jen's short, middle-age hairstyle and wrinkles around her eyes and mouth reminded me I was up there in years, as well, though I still wore my hair long like a younger woman. Or a woman who never grew up. Seeing the bloated face of Lance Mewling on TV was an even starker reminder of our age.

"What got him fired from the TV station?" I asked.

"Holocaust denial. He only hinted at it in his on-air commentaries, but it turns out, he has this big conspiracy-theory website. There are tons of videos of him going way off the deep end. A history professor at the college teamed up with the Anti-Defamation League to get him fired, along with his researcher."

"So what's he doing now?"

"He has a TV show that runs on the internet. Getting fired hasn't silenced him at all. He's worse than ever with his hate-mongering and wacky conspiracies."

"Is he really bitter about getting fired?"

Jen was about to take a sip of coffee, but put her cup down. "Do you think I actually watch his videos?"

"No. Sorry. I just figured if he was angry, he'd be ranting about it online."

"Why are you asking about him, anyway?"

I couldn't tell her anything about the Memory Guild. None of the "normal" people in the city knew about it and never would. So I fibbed a little.

"I know the professor who got Mewling fired," I said. "He's been getting death threats. I'm worried about him."

"That's what the police are for. You know, Mewling doesn't

have to threaten the professor. He only needs to say bad things about him, and his rabid followers will make the threats."

That was true. But it expanded our list of suspects a thousand-fold.

"What do you know about Mewling's personal life?" I asked, hoping to find another angle to pursue.

"Well." She smiled with a self-satisfied look. "I have heard rumors he's been cheating on his third wife. And his drinking has been out of control. Some say he's amassed an arsenal of weapons in his home, which, I heard, might go on the market soon. He's greatly in debt, too, despite raking in millions."

"Boy, he sounds like a powder keg about to explode."

"He does, indeed. These are great muffins, by the way."

"Don't change the subject," I said. "What's Mewling's vulnerability? How could I leverage information from him?"

"Well, he's on his third marriage. In his last divorce, his wife took him to the cleaners. So he's surely reluctant to get another one. His current wife has probably heard some of the rumors about him having a mistress. But if she got unquestionable evidence of the affair—the kind that makes her look bad if she looked the other way—then Mr. Mewling would be in a very bad place."

That was exactly the type of sleaziness I wanted nothing to do with. So I changed the subject. We talked about the muffins until Jen had to meet a client to show a house.

I RETURNED TO THE INN JUST BEFORE NOON. I WAS STARTLED to find Archibald attached to the subway tile above the stove.

"Hello, Archibald. What brings you in here?"

"I needed to speak to you as soon as you returned. I have terrible news."

My stomach turned cold. Lately, bad news has been of only one kind: deadly.

"Gloria has been harmed," he said, with a glitch of grief in his throat that was extra touching coming from a gargoyle. "The assassins tried again, and this time they almost succeeded."

I reached behind me to catch myself, as I crumbled against the counter.

"What—how?"

"She was nearly strangled to death, or so I heard through the supernatural network. Strangled in her shop. She was saved by a client coming in and interrupting the assassin just in the nick of time. She's at the hospital in intensive care. The police have already finished gathering evidence in her shop."

"What is the Guild going to do?"

"I'll let you know as soon as I find out."

I was devastated. Gloria was such a sweet woman who would harm no one. What sort of monster would try to kill her?

"I don't know anything about her family," I said. "Have they been notified?"

"She has a daughter who lives in town. She has been told, I believe."

"Can Gloria take visitors?"

"Not while she's still in the ICU."

The chime went off from the front door opening. A thing that should happen often in an inn filled with guests. Mine was not.

The bell rang at the front desk. The stereotypical bell that's round and squat and you slap it with your hand. Either a new guest was checking in, of which none was expected, or a package needed a signature. Again, none was expected. Otherwise, it meant bad news.

I left the kitchen and entered the foyer. Detective Lepore was waiting. A uniformed officer stood behind her.

Uh-oh.

"Hello, Ms. Chesswick," she said with a fake smile.

"Uh, hi?"

"Can you come with us to the station to make a statement?"

"A statement about what?"

"I'm sorry to inform you that Gloria Salter has been assaulted."

I couldn't pretend to be surprised.

"I just found out about this myself," I said. "I can't think of a statement that would be helpful."

"I want you to answer a few questions. That would be helpful."

"Why me?"

"Well, for one, your fingerprints were found all over the place. And you had a guest here who was just murdered. Your fingerprints were found on glassware that held her fingerprints, as well."

"Wait a minute. Am I a suspect?"

"We can't divulge that. All I can say is that you're a person of interest."

"Are you arresting me?" I asked.

"Not at the moment. I'm asking you to make an appearance voluntarily. If you refuse, then it's a different story."

"Okay," I said. "I'll come with you."

I felt like I was in a nightmare. The kind you can't simply wake up from.

CHAPTER 7

UNDER ATTACK

"I don't see how a few fingerprints make me a 'person of interest,'" I said to Detective Lepore as we walked to her car parked on the street outside of my inn. The uniformed police officer kept a discreet distance. Her patrol car was visible on the next block.

"That's for us and the prosecutor to decide."

I had caught Julie before she left early for the day. She didn't have many rooms to clean, after all. I asked her to stay long enough to serve the afternoon tea and to check in a new guest who was due to arrive. (Yes, an actual new guest!) So, I was covered, in case I was at the station for a long time.

"I actually have to get in the back seat, like I'm being arrested?" I asked with more of a whiny tone than I intended.

"My laptop stand takes up too much room in the front seat," Lepore said. She was exaggerating. There was room in the front seat for someone. I'm sure Samson had sat there many a time.

There wasn't a plexiglass barrier between the front and back seats like you find in patrol cars and taxis. I figured the back seat wasn't so bad after all. The car was an unmarked Ford. My nosy neighbors wouldn't know it was a cop car and hopefully, hadn't noticed the uniformed officer.

"I hope you're not going to handcuff me," I said.

"I wasn't planning on it, but if you keep giving me a hard time, I will."

As I got into the car, which still smelled new, I had a frightening thought: what if they arrested me? How could I run my inn from the county jail? I'd have to be like an imprisoned drug lord passing instructions to subordinates.

And another scary thought popped up: Esmeralda was in the county jail. The women's wing wasn't that large, so I wouldn't be able to avoid her. She would beat me up. Maybe even shiv me, if that was the correct term. I wasn't really up on jail slang.

"Should I get a lawyer?" I asked as Lepore slid into the driver's seat.

"You have the right to, but you don't need one. We're just going to chat."

I didn't know any lawyers to call. The lawyer I used when I divorced Buddy wouldn't be any help.

Lepore started the car and pulled out onto Cadiz Street. There wasn't any traffic. There rarely was, except for residents and the occasional tourist trolley. As the car rolled down the narrow street, I realized I was in all intents and purposes in Lepore's custody.

Lepore cursed.

I looked up and saw a black muscle car headed toward us, the wrong way along the one-way street.

Lepore stopped and honked her horn. The black car did, too. She lowered her window, stuck her head out, and shouted to the driver that he was going the wrong way.

A male passenger got out of the passenger seat and walked

toward us. He was dressed all in black, and his head and face were covered by a black balaclava.

My insides froze.

Lepore switched on a row of flashing lights mounted on the inside of the windshield, next to the roof. Her hand moved to her holster.

The man ran toward our car. But he wasn't headed for Lepore. He ran around the passenger side and pulled a gun from under his shirt.

He aimed it at me.

Lepore gunned the engine and threw the car in reverse, swinging the front of the car around to the left.

The gunman fired once, twice. The passenger-side rear window shattered. But the gunman had to jump out of the way to avoid getting hit by the rear of Lepore's car.

The car shuddered as she hit a parked car. She drove forward onto the opposite sidewalk, almost hitting a fire hydrant. Then, she reversed. The gunman, aiming again, had to dodge us before he got his shot off.

Now, Lepore took off down the street in the opposite direction, approaching my inn. Two more gunshots. I couldn't tell if they hit anything.

Lepore was on the radio requesting back up. The patrol car that had come with her finally appeared, driving around the block to cut the black car off from behind. The gunman ran off into an alley.

But his driver hadn't given up. The black car was following us, quickly catching up.

Lepore turned onto Hidalgo Avenue, vibrating over its cobblestones.

"Are you okay?" she asked me.

"Yeah. I hope I didn't pee myself."

"I thought he was going to shoot me. But he was coming for you."

The car lurched. The black car had rammed us from behind.

"I don't think he knew I was a cop until I turned my strobes on. But that didn't stop him."

There was traffic on this two-way street, and Lepore did a good job of passing cars. But the black car kept up to us. The shimmering waters of the bay appeared ahead. The avenue was about to take a sharp bend to the left as it reached the bay. I turned, expecting to see the black car bail out of the chase.

But the car shot past us. What a maniac! He was going to cut us off again.

Just then, a police car with flashing lights rounded the bend ahead towards us. It turned into the path of the black car which braked and swerved to avoid the collision.

The black car bounced onto the sidewalk and crashed into an antique lamp post with a banner encouraging tourists to "relive history." The post toppled over onto the roof of the car.

The officer in the police cruiser raced to the black car, gun drawn. The one who had accompanied Lepore to the inn appeared and joined him. Soon, they had the black-clad driver face down on the cobblestones, hands cuffed behind his back.

Lepore got out and joined the chaotic scene as more officers showed up. She spoke to one of them who looked like a supervisor.

I sat in the car and watched the scene. I checked and, no, I had not peed myself. Two officers grabbed the bad guy to his feet and led him to a police car parked nearby. The driver's door of the black car remained open. I got an idea.

The door handle didn't work, so I reached through the blown-out window and opened the door from outside. No one noticed me. So I casually strolled to the black car. At that moment, no officers were near it. I did something that could get me in trouble, but I did it anyway.

I bent over and reached into the black car, placing both my hands on the steering wheel.

It held a lot of adrenaline, fear, and anger. Dominating all the sensory input was hatred and resentment. It rose from the steering wheel like fumes. And there was a lot more energy here. I—

—got to kill her myself now. Dalton couldn't hit the side of a barn with that expensive gun he's so proud of. Did the cop clip him? Okay, I've got this . . . just need to get close enough to put one round in her head . . . oh, darn, now what? I'll kill the cop, too, if I have to. Now, ugh—

—I forced my mind to rise above the immediacy of the thug's thoughts he had while chasing us. I needed to find earlier memories to understand who these assassins were. Here, I sensed powerful feelings. I dove into—

—the Truth Squad. I mean, like, I believe in our mission, but is it all just B.S. to get us to kill people for free? I mean, don't get me wrong, I would gladly kill for Him. Gladly lay down my own life. God has chosen Him, and I am his soldier. But I don't understand why we kill some of the people we do. They don't seem to be His enemies. But there are always hidden truths, and He knows the truth more than us. Yeah, I know, I get it. That's why we're called the Truth Squad. We cut through the layers of deceit. But, I have to admit, I feel kind of funny taking out a little middle-aged innkeeper. I mean, what kind of harm is she doing? Yeah, I know, she's part of the cabal. She just doesn't look like it, is what I'm saying. I'm glad you're the triggerman on this job. I can't blow away a lady that looks like my Aunt Mary. So, yeah, I know. And do it quick, and we'll—

—I heard my name, yanking me out of the driver's thoughts.

"I said, please take your hands from the wheel and step away from the car, Ms. Chesswick."

It was Detective Lepore, pushing her way into my space.

"Yeah, sorry," I said. "I was having a brain fart."

"Why were you holding the steering wheel?" she asked. "This isn't a used car lot."

Apparently, Samson hadn't told her about my abilities.

"I don't know," I said. "Maybe it's a post-traumatic therapy. Like grabbing the horns of the bull that almost gored you."

Her face said she didn't believe me. I tried to change the subject.

"What happened to the shooter?" I asked.

"They'll find him. I think I clipped him with my car, so he can't run very fast. We're cordoning off the immediate area. He won't get far."

As if to illustrate her point, a helicopter passed us slowly overhead. I didn't know the San Marcos Police Department even had a helicopter.

"Do you have any idea why someone would try to kill you?" she asked.

I couldn't tell her about the Memory Guild, so I stretched some facts.

"I think someone has a grudge against Professor Sven Noordlun," I said. "There was an attempt on his life the other day—trying to force him off the Segovia Street bridge. Gloria Salter was friends with him, and she was almost murdered. And I'm his friend, too. I believe Monique Simpson stayed at my inn planning to kill me. I caught her sneaking into my cottage in the middle of the night. I think she was murdered because she failed in her mission. And now, another attempt was made on my life. I've already talked to Detective Samson about this."

"I'm the lead on the Simpson homicides," Leper said in a flat voice. Talk to *me* first."

"All righty."

"Since you're so full of theories, why do you believe the professor is a target?"

I decided to throw all caution to the wind.

"Lance Mewling. Professor Noordlun is a historian, you know, and he led a campaign against Mewling for being a Holocaust denier. Mewling got fired from his TV job. That sounds like a good motive to me."

"Maybe to hurt the professor. Not to kill his random friends."

"Who are you calling random?"

"You obviously have lots of thoughts to share," Lepore said. "Let's continue our chat at the station."

"You still suspect me? Even after someone just tried to kill me?"

"I'm just being methodical. Please get back in my car."

"Yes, Detective Leper."

"*Lepore*. This is getting old."

And another thing bugged me: I look like the driver's Aunt Mary? Does that mean old?

LEPORE KEPT ME AT THE STATION UNTIL HER SHIFT ENDED IN the early evening. I think she did it just to punish me for my attitude and for going around her and speaking with Samson. Out of the nearly five hours I spent there, only one was spent with her, in a formal interview that was recorded on video. It was a rehash of questions she had already asked me, such as my whereabouts when Monique and Gloria were attacked. If she wanted to do everything by the book, fine, she could waste my time.

But as I whiled the hours away in a plastic chair in the

hallway outside of the detective bureau, I searched the internet on my phone, looking for tidbits on Mewling. I wanted to see if he was the vengeful type. And I was curious if he was the "He" the bad guy was talking or thinking about while his hands were on the steering wheel.

The more I looked, the more I saw of a cultish world of conspiracies and grievances revolving around a cult of personality created by Lance Mewling.

The former television commentator was quite busy without his TV job. His website, "The Truth Zone," was filled with drivel about evil governments, nefarious plots, and Lizard People taking over the planet. But it was effectively drivel. All his videos had thousands, if not millions, of views. His articles and blog posts each had a mile-long string of reader comments.

Reading those comments made my spine tingle. Because seeded throughout were sentiments that sounded like what the assassin's driver had been thinking: that *He* was the instrument of God and I, the commentator, will do whatever it takes to serve Him.

That's scary stuff. What was it about Mewling that inspired such devotion?

The more I read, and the more videos I watched, I realized Mewling was a genius at pandering to people's paranoias, hatreds, fears, jealousies, prejudices—pretty much all the bad emotions that motivate bad things.

And I had to admit that Mewling was a charismatic fellow. He wasn't handsome in my opinion, but he had the classic square-jawed anchorman face and the rich baritone voice. When he was just a newscaster, I liked his old-school gravitas. Once he became a commentator, his smooth, stentorian delivery was so pleasing to the ear, you often overlooked how wacky his views were. When he went over the edge into conspiracy land, I stopped taking him seriously. But his followers never got over his hypnotic voice and square jaw.

And as he moved into crazy land, his fanbase exploded. He was no longer just a star in a small television market; he went national. Politicians feted him. Dangerous extremists cozied up to him.

I had to admit that getting Mewling fired didn't hurt his career at all. It probably helped it.

So was there any reason for him to target the Memory Guild? I couldn't think of one other than spite for his firing. True, getting canned must have been humiliating, but, again, it didn't harm his fame or fortune.

After Lepore finally gave me permission to go home, a thought occurred to me as I rode in a taxi through the darkened ancient city.

Mewling knew Dr. Noordlun was an enemy. But he didn't know Gloria, and he wouldn't have remembered me from high school. I overstated our relationships to the professor when I spoke to Lepore. Our only connection to him was the Guild. So Mewling would have to know about the Memory Guild.

But how would he know? The Guild's existence was a secret, except to the other supernatural guilds and a few select allies in the non-supernatural population. It was a vexing hole in my theory. If I could find out for sure he knew about the Guild, it would make my theory look a lot better.

When I went inside the inn, I heard familiar voices coming from the kitchen. It made me angry.

Archibald and resident vampire Roderick were playing chess. The gargoyle was affixed to the subway tile above one of the counters, which held the chessboard within reach of his tiny claws.

"I told you guys to be discreet when guests are here."

"You barely have any guests, I shouldn't have to remind you," Roderick said, "and they're asleep or watching TV in their rooms at the moment."

I gave the vampire, in his nineteenth-century clothing and long, wavy hair, an icy stare.

"What?" he asked. "I wasn't stalking them."

"Yeah. You sure as heck know better than that. But do keep your voices down. Even though the kitchen is off limits to guests, one could always wander in here."

"I'm sorry I don't spend my entire existence hidden away in my crawlspace so as not to be a bother," Roderick said.

"Like you were before I discovered you and removed the seal that kept you imprisoned there."

"True, and I appreciate that. The fact is, tourist town or not, San Marcos goes to bed early. I have to do my hunting early in the evening. Is it really so bad for me to enjoy a little post-dinner companionship?"

I sighed.

"It seems neither of you are aware that I was almost killed today."

"Heavens, no!" Roderick said.

"Yes, I'm aware," Archibald said, moving a bishop. "Check."

"You don't seem too concerned."

"I am. But I'm stony faced. It comes with being a gargoyle."

"And with a heart of stone, too, I should say," Roderick muttered.

"I'm quite happy you survived," Archibald said, fixing me with his baleful demon-like eyes. "The Guild has been beset with non-stop emergencies. James was also attacked today."

"Oh, no!"

"He had just finished a blacksmithing demonstration at the

Colonial reenactment village, when a man grabbed a pike replica and tried to impale him."

"Is James okay?"

"Thankfully, he is fine. It did not go well for the attacker, though. James broke the pike shaft over the man's head, and the fellow ended up with his butt roasting in the forge's fire. Can you believe James actually got reprimanded for attacking a paying customer?"

"Have the police identified him?" I asked.

"Dr. Noordlun said the man had only minor arrests on his record and no known criminal gang affiliations."

"Who are these people?" It didn't make sense to me.

"Loosely affiliated crazies who fancy themselves to be assassins," Archibald said.

"I spoke to Esmerelda in the county jail. I don't believe she's behind this. Right now, the more I learn about Lance Mewling, the more I can imagine him instigating it. But his firing didn't harm him enough for him to want to wipe out the Guild in retaliation. And how would he even know the Guild exists?"

Archibald stuck out his tongue and shrugged in an impish, gargoyle-like manner.

"We have a lot of work to do," he said.

"What about the others the Guild has thwarted?" I asked. "The treasure hunter is another person who doesn't seem to have a reason to harm us. Has anything been learned about him?"

"He's had his hands full with his own problems. His treasure museum was recently broken into and ransacked."

"What about the other possibilities?"

"Alas, there are many, many others. The Guild is quite good at thwarting."

"And not so good at protecting yourselves," Roderick said.

"I wonder if the other guilds could help us," I said. "Like the Vampire Guild."

"You know I'll have nothing to do with them," Roderick said. "They're the ones who sealed me in the crawlspace for eternity. Until you came along."

"What did you do exactly?" Archibald asked.

"Nothing serious enough to deserve that punishment. Non-payment of dues. And the small matter of preying on my guests when I owned this inn. Bad for tourism, you see."

"I don't want to be attacked again," I said. "And I'm tired of waiting around for that to happen. We need to go on the offensive."

"But against whom?" Archibald asked, frustrated.

I didn't have an answer, other than, "The bad guys."

Archibald turned his attention back to the chess match as Roderick moved his king out of harm's way.

Then I got an idea of a way to search for the bad guys.

CHAPTER 8

SLAY HIM

It was still early enough in the night to call James. He picked up on the fourth ring.

"Custom Metal Fabrication. This is James."

As a metal-speaker, it wasn't surprising that working with metal was James' passion and career. Whether it was making custom railings for clients or demonstrating how the sixteenth-century Spanish blacksmiths worked, James was finely tuned to all types of metal and could coax them into revealing their secrets of when they were made and what history they were involved in.

"Hi James, it's Darla. Are you okay?"

He laughed, but it didn't sound sincere. "Of course I am."

"You're not injured?"

"Nope. But the other guy was. I made sure of that."

"What set him off to attack you?"

"I don't know. It was at the end of my demonstration. The audience was leaving. A few people came up to ask me questions, and I saw them suddenly look at something behind me. The guy had grabbed one of the pikes I have on display and lunged at me. He could have skewered me really bad if I hadn't dodged quick enough. When he missed, I grabbed the shaft and got it away from him pretty easily. Then I showed him who's boss."

"Did he say anything?"

"When he lunged at me, he called me a traitor. But he didn't say anything after I drubbed him, even when the police questioned him."

"What did he look like?"

"Like an angry nerd, if you know what I mean. Skinny, glasses, clean-shaven. Camouflage pants and black sweatshirt. Baseball cap with the word 'truth' on it. After his hat was knocked off, I saw he had a buzz cut. He seemed like a military wannabe."

"Did the police take the pike as evidence?"

"I see where you're going. They took the business end, the metal head, above where the shaft was broken. But they left the butt behind, where the guy was holding it. You might be able to get a reading from it."

"Excellent. Can I come by tomorrow?"

"Sure. Come before we're open to the public. I'm usually there at eight to get the fire going. You know, one other strange detail. When the police arrested the guy, they found he had a concealed handgun. Why didn't he just shoot me instead of trying to impale me with the pike?"

"Maybe he thought impaling you would send a more horrifying message to the rest of us," I suggested.

"Yeah, maybe. Good thing his ammo didn't go off when I tossed his butt in the fire."

"I need to warn you, James, that things are truly getting dangerous for us. I was attacked earlier today."

"Holy Moses! What happened?"

I gave him the brief version of the ambush and shooting.

"Please stay safe," he said. "Do you have a gun?"

"No, but I have a new alarm system."

"I wish you had a gun."

"We'll see about that."

A racing mind wouldn't let me sleep, so I got on my laptop and dove deep into the foul swamps of the internet. First, I explored Lance Mewling's website in more depth, skimming through the countless comments that were left beneath his blog posts and videos. If he had hired the assassins, this could be where they were recruited.

The more time I spent on Mewling's site, the more I realized his primary purpose in life was self-aggrandizement. He draped himself in the cloak of patriotism, claiming he fought to save the country from everything that wasn't red-blooded Americana. But all his writings and videos circled around to praising himself and promoting his latest book.

I noticed he was careful to speak about fighting his enemies only in the political sense, never with actual violence. But his followers made that connection all on their own. Many commenters professed to be a member of this or that militia group and boasted about fighting America's enemies, though they gave no specifics. The only exception were calls to appear at various political rallies or protests.

My eyes were tired from scanning text on my screen. But then they seized upon three special words:

The Truth Squad

That, I believed, was the name of the group of assassins.

A commenter had asked where he could get more information on The Truth Squad. Someone replied that it was a forbidden topic on this site, but there was a channel on the 8kun message board where he could submit his contact info, if he wanted to join the squad.

I went to the site. I've heard it categorized as part of the "dark web." The primitive, low-design site was filled with dark matter: racist and sexist rants, calls for violence.

I found the board for The Truth Squad. But slammed my hand on the table in frustration. The board was password protected.

Too bad the Memory Guild didn't have a hacker in its membership. But at least I had found a connection, however slight, between Lance Mewling's followers and The Truth Squad.

I went to sleep with a baseball bat under my bed and my new burglar alarm system armed. Once all my adrenaline from the rollercoaster day drained away, I slept like a rock. Or, I should say, like a gargoyle.

San Marcos' Colonial Village was located just off the main tourist street. The two acres included three actual historic buildings from the sixteen and seventeen hundreds, plus replica buildings such as the smithy and a cooper's shop. At this early hour, the place was deserted of T-shirt-clad tourists and costume-clad re-enactors. It was peaceful beneath the canopies of large, ancient live oak trees.

James let me in at the gate, and we went straight to his smithy. It was open on three sides with a wooden roof above and a shed on the fourth side. Already, the coal fire of the forge was glowing.

James opened the shed, which was filled with blacksmith tools and iron pieces he had fabricated. He ducked inside and retrieved a smooth wooden shaft about the diameter of a shovel handle. It extended for about five feet from the butt to a jagged break. He handed it to me, and I was impressed by its heft.

"You broke this on the guy's head?" I asked. "I'm surprised he survived."

He chuckled. "I guess I'm lucky he did." He scratched his beard in thought. "You know, that blow should have knocked him out, but didn't. Now that I think about it, he was acting intense—much more than just a guy excited and scared. It was like he was on something. Amped up on drugs."

"Could be," I said. I cradled the pike shaft carefully in my hands, feeling the crackling of energy in the wood. "Can I sit down somewhere?"

James pointed to a small bleacher-like seating area of three tiered benches. I climbed to the middle bench and got comfortable. Then I slid both hands along the shaft, listening to the breeze rattle the oak leaves above me. Soon, I imagined hearing voices of tourists who weren't there and the clangs of a hammer striking metal atop the anvil. I—

—am standing at the edge of the crowd, beside the storage shed. It's not a good angle to see what the blacksmith is doing, because he has his back to me. But I can just walk up to him and put a round in the back of his head. The spectators will run, and I can just stroll out of here. I reach for my gun, but there's that buzzing in my ears again. My head is throbbing. STOP IT. Leave me alone! I'm going to kill him, okay? No, I have to smite him? What the heck does smite mean? Oh, I have to slay him. I understand that word. I have to do it in the traditional manner, you say? Why? Stop that, it hurts! Okay, okay, I will obey. I will slay him in the manner that men have slain each other since the dawn of time. Yes, I will pierce his heart, but please stop the pain.

Look, there leaning against the shed are old-fashioned weapons like swords, muskets, and spears. No, not spears, they're pikes. My eyes are locked upon one of them, taller than I am, its metal point is long and sharp . . . okay, I will obey you—I will drive this weapon into the back of the traitor who is thine enemy . . . I step into the smithy and grab the wooden shaft that feels right in my hands. I aim the point at the large man's back, and it's as if I see a target there between his shoulder blades, and I lunge toward him, the pike in both hands, horizontal at my side. Gasping sounds come from the crowd as time slows down, and my arms flex as I thrust the—

—jarring, confusing images of violence and pain and I found myself lying on the plank beneath the bench I'd been sitting on.

"Are you okay?" James asked. He stood at the end of the bench looking at me with concern.

A brief clatter rose from below. The pike shaft hit the support beams below me as it fell to the ground.

"Yeah, I'm fine," I said, pulling myself onto the bench again. My head was spinning more slowly now as I gradually regained my equilibrium.

"I take it you had a vision of his memories."

"Oh, boy, I sure did." I slid to the edge of the bench, and James lent a hand to help me to the ground. I stood a little unsteadily.

"I take it his memory was powerful."

"Yeah, and not what I expected. I'd read the memories of the woman who checked into my inn to kill me, but she had lost her nerve. Yesterday, I read the memories of one of the men who tried to kill me when I was in the detective's car. But he was the driver, not the intended trigger man. After we escaped the shooter, the driver tried to cut us off, but didn't have a specific plan to kill me. Now, this today," I pointed to the shaft on the ground, "this is the first time I read the thoughts of an assassin who was about to kill one of us."

"And?"

"It was as if some other consciousness was in his mind, influencing him. I couldn't sense this other entity, only the guy's reactions to it. But the odd thing is, he was planning on shooting you until the entity forced him to use the pike."

"That's bizarre," James said, stroking his beard. "Why would it do that?"

"Something about it being the traditional, age-old way of smiting your enemy."

"Who says 'smite' anymore?"

"Apparently, the entity said it to our guy."

"I guess it's an ancient entity."

"Yeah," I said. "And ancient usually means scary and powerful."

I thanked James, and we said goodbye by telling each other to be extra careful. Watching out for an army of conspiracy nuts was hard enough, but throw in an evil, ancient entity, and what's a girl to do?

And, furthermore, what was the connection between Mewling's followers and the entity? There was no mention of anything supernatural on his website or social media.

The only logical conclusion was that James' assailant personally had an evil, ancient-entity problem or, more likely, was schizophrenic.

I was about to call Samson to ask what was known about the assailant, but remembered Lepore was peeved that I had gone around her before. Instead, I called the personal number she had given me. She didn't answer.

So, I called Samson.

"I was told I wasn't supposed to speak to you directly," Samson said.

"I called Leper first—"

"Lepore."

"Right, I tried her first, and she wouldn't take my call. You're next on the list. Besides, we're friends. I'm allowed to call my friends."

"We are?"

"I'm hurt that you'd question that."

"Okay, Miss Chesswick—"

"Darla."

"Right. What do you need?"

"Do you have the name of the person who attacked James Birken at the Colonial Village yesterday?" I asked.

"How do you know about that? It hasn't come out in the news yet."

"I'm an acquaintance of James." I was as vague as I could be.

"Let me see . . . the perp's name is Jeffrey Whittle. No priors."

"Was he put under observation for drug use or mental disorders while in custody?"

"Um, no mention of that."

"Do you know if there's any connection between him and Lance Mewling?"

"Whoa, whoa! Hold on a minute. You're getting way ahead of yourself. Why would there be any connection? Why would we even think there would be?"

"I had mentioned to your good friend Detective Le-*pore* that Mewling might seek retribution against Dr. Sven Noordlun, who's also an acquaintance of James and mine. And of Gloria Salter."

"Retribution, as in murder?"

"Possibly."

"For what?"

"Getting him fired from Channel Nine," I said.

"Man, that's a real stretch. A public figure is going to risk everything to kill a bunch of people for allegedly getting him fired from a job he doesn't need?"

When he put it that way, it did sound far-fetched.

"Are you still there?" he asked.

"All I can say is my acquaintances and I are being targeted. Gloria was almost murdered. And you heard what happened to me yesterday?"

"Yeah, Cynthia told me."

So, on a first-name basis? Of course.

"Well, I'm trying to come up with theories why," I said. "What are you doing?"

"Look, we don't just sit around and come up with theories. We collect evidence and statements. We use them to determine suspects and motives."

"So whatcha got, then?"

He sighed with exasperation.

"I'm not at liberty to say. And let me ask you the questions now. Why are you acquainted with this very diverse group of individuals?"

"I grew up in this city. I have many acquaintances."

"Why would you be working with a history professor, a psychic, and a blacksmith to get a TV commentator fired?"

"Because he's a Holocaust denier."

"Yeah, but why are you working with *these* random people?"

"We're just people who care about the truth."

"Yeah, I'm sure. And . . . please hold."

He put me on mute. Then he came back on.

"Detective Lepore would like to speak to you," he said.

Her voice came over the line, "What did I tell you about going around me?"

"Sorry. You weren't taking my calls."

"You called once, only about five minutes ago."

"Sorry. I guess I get too impatient."

"Look, Ms. Chesswick, I've assigned officers to keep an eye on your inn. At this point, there's nothing you can do. Let us do the police work. You only need to stay safe."

"May I suggest other acquaintances of mine who could use some officers keeping an eye out for them?"

"What do you mean?"

"I have a group of acquaintances. Of whom, three others besides myself have been attacked. The others are surely next."

I rattled off the names of the other human guild members: Gloria, James, Summer, Laurel, Dr. Noordlun, and Diana. I didn't include Diego, who could probably hold his own as a vampire. Sage was dead already. Archibald was also supernatural and lived with me.

"Have they been threatened?" Leper, I mean, Lepore asked.

"Three have been attacked, and the rest surely will be threatened."

"What is it all these acquaintances have in common, other than being your acquaintances?"

"Collaborating in the effort to get Lance Mewling fired."

"Not that crackpot theory again," she said.

"Yep. That one. Why won't you take it seriously?"

"I spoke to Mr. Mewling myself regarding the attack on Dr. Noordlun. Mr. Mewling categorically denies any knowledge of a plot against the professor or of even knowing who he is."

"Of course he'll deny it," I said.

"We can't go any further until we find evidence or witnesses tying Mr. Mewling to the attack."

Yeah, it looked like I was the one who was going to have to find them.

"But Ms. Chesswick," Lepore said, "I'll get statements from the 'acquaintances' on your list and then determine if they need protection."

"Thank you, Detective. Now let me speak to—"

The line went dead.

I PONDERED WHAT TO DO. THEN, I REMEMBERED WHAT JEN had told me: Mewling was rumored to be having an affair. If I could obtain proof of that, I could threaten to make it public unless he admitted sending The Truth Squad against us. I admit it was a scummy strategy to use. But, you know, killing people was even scummier, so I had a long way to sink before I got down to Mewling's level.

The tactic I would use wasn't clever at all. It was the standard one used by private detectives hired to find out if a spouse was cheating: staking out the suspect's home and following him around.

I had an inn to run, so I could spend only so many hours sitting in a car waiting for something to happen while needing to pee. But I had supernatural acquaintances who could help. Sage had been missing in action ever since Gloria was almost killed. But Diego, the vampire, would be excellent for nighttime surveillance, plus he had superhuman senses. Maybe Archibald could help, too, though I wasn't sure how.

Between the three of us, we would find out if Mewling was sneaking off to a forbidden rendezvous, or if his mistress was sneaking into his mansion where his video studio was.

The only weak part of my plan was recruiting my partners. Archibald was not the sort to be told what to do. I'd have to convince him it was his idea.

And Diego was a special challenge. I hardly knew him since I was such a new member of the Guild.

And you never, ever want to get a vampire angry.

CHAPTER 9

LOVE SCONES

My phone buzzed with a text message. I hoped it was a Guild member or Samson with new information.

No, it was from my daughter, Sophie.

"Mom, I need $600 tonight. I promise this will be the last time. Love you!" the text read.

I stewed. Every time she asked for money, it was allegedly the last time. Sometimes, she promised to pay me back. She never did. I guess mothers are merely sponges to be squeezed until they are dry, and squeezed again the moment they regain some moisture.

I didn't text back. I called her instead. She didn't answer, of course. With texts, you could avoid the hard questions, unlike with a phone call.

I was too indulgent with Sophie during her adolescence, when her father and I divorced. She fell into a bad crowd in high school and, unfortunately, went to college in San Marcos, making it too easy to stay with that crowd.

Her minor flirtations with drugs grew more serious. I sent

her to an expensive recovery center in South Florida, but she left voluntarily or was kicked out—the story always changed. She ended up with a sleazy operation that scammed insurance companies, and they sold her to a clan of vampires who intended to treat her like livestock.

My cousin, Missy, helped rescue Sophie. After all the trauma she experienced, I kept on indulging her, hoping she'd get her act together. Handing her the money she requested, always allegedly for the last time.

I called my mother. Sophie had moved in with her while I was living in Key West with Cory, The Husband Who Bailed. Sophie was still in Mom's Victorian home/antiques store, trying to save money to get her own apartment.

I knew, any day now, my tiny two-bedroom cottage would have a new occupant who would promise it would only be temporary.

"Mom, what's the deal with Sophie?" I demanded the moment my mother answered her phone.

"Why? Is something wrong?"

"She texted me asking for money again. She didn't quit her job, did she?"

"I don't believe so. She complained she wanted to work more shifts, now that it's tourist season, but they already have too many servers there."

"Has she asked you for money?"

"No," Mom said. "Well, just twenty dollars last week."

I sighed. "She better not be on drugs again."

"You would know if you spent more time with her."

I'm a sucker for guilt. It works on me every time, from Mom and Sophie both.

"Why don't you stop by here this afternoon?" Mom asked.

"Things have been really hectic." That was my way of saying

two guests were just murdered here in one night, and someone tried to kill me yesterday.

"Just pop in for a cup of coffee. Sophie is working the lunch shift today and should be home in a half hour."

"Yeah, I'll see you then, but I have to get back here right afterwards to serve tea."

I was what marketers called the "sandwich generation." I had to look out for a kid (even though she was an adult), and a parent, while juggling a career. What do you call that sandwich when it also has to deal with murder and the supernatural? A sloppy joe?

In thirty minutes, I was sitting in Mom's cozy kitchen that hadn't been renovated since the 1960s but still was charming. Mom had the jet-black hair of the Chesswick women, though hers was frizzy, and Sophie's and mine were long and straight. Of course, Mom was using a heavy-duty dye job and an occasional magic spell to combat the gray hairs.

Ever since I discovered I was psychometric, I tried to avoid touching things in Mom's house other than coffee mugs and stirring spoons. You'd think an antiques store would be like a candy shop to a psychometrist, with so many eclectic objects holding layers of memories. But it's actually more like sensory overload.

Helping her unpack a box of knickknacks could send me on dozens of wild rides that I didn't necessarily want to experience, like being stuck at a party next to the retired guy who tries to tell you every story that occurred during his career. Maybe it's interesting for some folks, but not to me and not now.

And there's always the chance an object here could hold horrifying memories that I would have to relive. Let me tell you, it's not easy being a psychometrist.

Sitting at the table across from me, Mom was going on about some chair she had found on the side of the road. Oh, did I mention that Mom's shop was not a snooty high-end boutique? No, it was more of a junk store. She loved nothing more than finding nice pieces cheap at thrift stores—or free on the side of the road—and turning them around for a decent profit. She had a few valuable pieces, but this was not the place where rich customers and interior decorators shopped. At the moment, there weren't any customers in the shop at all.

Mom scooped dough for scones onto a sheet pan and slid it into the oven. Sophie's vintage Volkswagen Beetle pulled into the drive that went past the side of the house to a detached garage behind it. No one parked inside the garage, of course, since it was packed with junk.

"Hi Mom, hi Grammers," Sophie said when she entered the kitchen through the back door. She gave us each a kiss on the cheek.

Sophie was the prettiest of the Chesswick women. Not as petite as the generations before her, she was nevertheless thin with elfin features and milky white skin. I never got over the disappointment of seeing the tattoos creep inexorably up her pale, slender neck.

"Sophie, why do you need six hundred dollars?" I asked.

"Oh, did you bring it in cash?"

"No, I did not!"

She frowned with disappointment. "Do you have a money-transfer app?"

"You didn't answer me. Why do you need it?"

"To help a friend," she said, rummaging in the refrigerator, trying to avoid my gaze.

"You're not in the position to be generous to friends. Especially, since it's not your money."

"I'll pay you back," she said.

See, I told you this was coming.

"Honey." I tried to keep my voice warm. "I've put everything I own into the inn. And it's not making a profit yet. Why do you need to give money to your friend?"

"It's okay," she said, still averting my eyes. "No problem. I won't bother you again."

Of course, she would bother me again in a week or two, but I wouldn't point that out.

"Is your friend in some kind of trouble?" I asked. "Is it a health matter?"

"It's okay, Mom." She left the kitchen and went to sit at the shop's counter in what used to be the living room.

Nowadays, it seemed six hundred dollars couldn't take you very far. But it was still too much to be so casual about it. Sophie was being secretive, and it bothered me.

The afternoon teas at my inn are famous for my homemade scones. I bake them regularly, with blueberries, with cranberries, with raisins, and even with bits of chocolate. I serve them at breakfast sometimes, as well. It's a small touch, but guests love them and frequently mention them in their reviews on the booking websites.

But I'll give credit where it's due. My recipe came from Mom. She remains the sovereign of scones. I inhaled the buttery aroma as they baked in her oven.

The bell tinkled at the front door of her shop. Which used to be our family home before the countless antiques took over, and she began placing price tags on them.

Mom looked at her watch and smiled knowingly.

"Detective Reyna!" Sophie called out from the living room, "How are you this afternoon?"

"Whatcha got for me, kid?" he asked.

This was a thrice-weekly ritual. Detective Billy Reyna from the Property Crimes Division would stop by, ostensibly to inquire if any shady individuals tried to sell us hot merchandise. Of course, Mom would never accept stolen goods knowingly. But it could happen. Billy knew Mom had some unspecified psychic ability, and that I had the uncanny ability to learn things about the previous possessor of an object, and whether it was obtained through criminal means.

So, on the surface, these visits were business related.

But they always coincided with the time of day the scones came out of the oven.

Mom would offer Billy some scones. He would politely refuse. She'd press him harder. He'd relent and accept a small plate of the goodies, with jam and a cup of tea or coffee. Then, he'd admit the scones were the real reason he came by.

That was the ritual. It never changed.

"My, what a wonderful smell!" Billy said, entering the kitchen. He was an older man in his later sixties, with a big nose, thick eyeglasses, and an unruly head of curly white hair.

But I knew there was another ulterior motive for his visit. To flirt with Mom. The slightly younger widower was smitten with her. I believed the feeling was mutual, though Mom denied it.

"You look lovely today as usual," Billy said, though he was eying the oven, not Mom.

"They'll be ready in a few minutes," Mom said.

I contemplated the fact that Mom and I were probably the only parent-child team to both have flirting sessions with detectives from the same police force.

"I'm sorry about the tragedies at your inn," Billy said to me.

At first, I bristled hearing it out loud. But then I realized it was only natural that cops would be talking about the Simpsons' deaths in this small city with very few murders.

"Thank you," I said in a monotone.

"Do Samson and Lepore have any leads?" he asked.

"Nope," I said. "I thought you'd know the scuttlebutt more than I."

"I'm not privy to what the homicide detectives are up to."

"Well, those two detectives seem to be up to a lot," I said, fishing for information. "They make such a lovely couple. I mean, partners. They're just partners, right?"

Billy peered at me through his thick lenses. "There are rumors, but I wouldn't know anything about it," he said, carefully.

The old-fashioned, wind-up timer dinged. Mom opened the oven door, and an aroma of pure happiness filled the kitchen. Billy practically swooned.

Mom placed the baking sheet atop the stove to cool. "Don't go snatching any just yet," she said. "Tea or coffee?"

"I'll just pour myself a cup of joe from this pot," he said.

"But that's old. Let me make a fresh pot."

"Nothing wrong with old," he said. "Older is deeper and richer," he said with a suggestive smile.

"And more bitter," I added.

They ignored me, their courtship dance in full swing.

At times like this, I became suspicious about Mom's scone recipe. You see, Mom always had a reputation in the neighborhood for being an amateur witch. Old men would come to her for help in picking lottery numbers or for special powders to make their vegetable gardens produce more. Old ladies would come for balms to ease pain, or hexes to cause pain in abusive bosses.

Younger women would come to Mom for her scones. They were rumored to contain magic that caused men to fall in love.

That was years ago, before Mom became obsessed with selling antiques and allowed her hoarder instinct to take over. She was less active in offering her witchy services. And she swore her scones were now magic-free. In fact, they had always been, and how could such silly rumors have begun?

I wasn't so sure, as I watched Billy stand at the counter, spreading jam on a scone with a butter knife, his eyes alight with delight and fixed upon Mom.

I bit into a scone, still warm, slightly crunchy on the outside, soft and flaky on the inside. Nothing tasted of strange ingredients. No magic energy flooded my palate. But maybe, the magic wasn't meant to work on women.

Maybe, the magic was meant only for single men.

"Would you like some more?" Mom asked Billy.

"You bet I would."

Sophie walked into the kitchen. "Are there any scones left?" She glanced at the rapidly diminishing stock on the baking sheet.

"I'm about to do a second batch."

Sophie snatched one before it was too late.

"I thought these were for customers," she said with a full mouth. "To be set out on a plate as a sign of hospitality."

Everyone in the kitchen, including me, murmured in agreement. All of us with mouths full.

"The second batch is for customers," Mom said.

I glanced at my watch. It was time to head back to the inn. There was much work to do while I pretended two of my rooms were not, in fact, crime scenes.

"I should head back," I said.

"Me, too," Billy said, his mouth full once more.

Mom tore a sheet of foil and wrapped up four scones, handing the package to Billy.

"Thank you, Sadie," he said. "You spoil me."

He said goodbye to all of us and exited through the store. He didn't use the back door like the Chesswick women did. Who knows, someday he might.

Mom removed from the fridge a bowl of scone dough, but not the same bowl that produced the first batch.

"Mom, you aren't adding your love potion to the scones, are you?"

"Why would I do that?"

"Because you like to have men fawning over you. Like a certain widowed detective."

"Nonsense. Why would I want someone who comes here every other day and never buys anything?"

Her emphasis on the last three words, not mine.

CHAPTER 10

DOING THE DEVIL'S WORK

Gloria had been moved from the Intensive Care Unit. She lay in the hospital bed with a broken nose, two black eyes, and a neck mottled with bruises. I tried to hide my shocked expression, but she noticed it anyway and smiled.

"I could use a little concealer," she said, "but the nurses don't dispense makeup."

I gave her a light kiss atop her head on her silver hair.

"I'm so sorry for what happened," I said. "You must be in so much pain."

"They do dispense some things to take care of pain. I'm feeling better."

"What happened? The police wouldn't tell me anything. In fact, they're treating me like a suspect."

"You? Why on earth?"

"The fingerprints I left in your shop the last time I was there. Your security camera was disabled, so they don't have much evidence."

"Yes. He spray-painted the camera lens. Like I knew he would."

"Of course."

"I had a premonition of the attack," she said, her eyes looking dreamy. "It came to me while I was doing paperwork. I saw it exactly the way it unfolded: He rang the bell like a walk-in. When I buzzed him in, he pulled on a ski mask, painted over the lens, then demanded my cash. I unlocked the box for him, but I knew his true intentions. He punched me in the face, and when I fell to the floor, he jumped on me and started strangling me. Then, a client arrived, banged on the door, and he ran away. The police just missed him."

"How did you call the police? Do you have a silent alarm?"

"No. I called them before the attack, right after I had my vision. I knew my premonition was of an event that was imminent, so I called nine-one-one right away and said the guy had already broken in."

"Of course. Did you get a good look at him?"

"He was a small guy, Caucasian, a wiry little monkey with a shaved head."

"You told the police it was definitely a man?"

"I most certainly did."

"Then why would Lepore suspect me?" I was kind of small and wiry, but come on, no one ever mistook me for a man. A monkey, maybe, but not a man.

"They're only pretending to suspect you. They just wanted to question you more since so much violence is happening in your orbit."

"You saw this in a vision?"

"Not a vision. A hypothesis."

"Of course. I guess that makes sense. Since Detective Lepore insisted on interviewing me, even though someone had just tried to shoot me right in front of her."

Also, Lepore seemed to like me just as much as I liked her. I bet she felt the sexual tension between her boyfriend and me. So, why not make my life miserable?

"Gloria, may I do a reading of you?" I asked.

"Of me? I'm not an inanimate object. Even though that little monkey man tried to turn me into one."

I smiled. "I never read a person before, except with my telepathy. When it works. But I'm hoping this man left a memory on your neck. I'll try not to hurt you."

"Go ahead."

I rested the fingertips of both hands, spread out upon her bruised, swollen neck. I tried to touch as lightly as I could to avoid causing more pain. And without looking like I was going to finish the job of strangling her, if a nurse happened to come in. Her skin was hot and slightly moist with an ointment. I kept my fingers still and—

—sadness, this is so wrong, I can't believe I'm doing this. She's a tool of the devil, right? Telling fortunes and spreading lies. Practicing the occult is evil. This is the Devil's work, so it's only proper that she takes the punishment . . . so why do I feel so guilty? This is wrong . . . I did not want to be forced to do this. But I feel like I've been brainwashed . . . hold still, and it'll be less painful for you . . . darn, she's strong for an old lady . . . maybe I have the Devil in me. Maybe it's me who's doing the Devil's work. Stop struggling, lady, let me put you out of your misery. Oh, no, someone's banging on the door! Is there a back exit? Got to—

—the memory faded.

I felt sick to my stomach. It had felt like I was strangling Gloria herself, and now I had guilt about it, just like the attacker.

"What's wrong?" Gloria asked. "You just went ten shades paler."

"Yeah. I went through his experience of strangling you. I feel like I owe you an apology."

She laughed nervously, then winced at the throat pain.

"He felt regret and guilt about trying to kill you," I said.

"Good. He ought to."

"No, really. It was as if he was being forced to do it against his will. Not what you'd expect a murderer to feel during the act. You know, I read the thoughts of the driver for the guy who tried to shoot me, and there's a common theme of being compelled in some unnatural way to act for someone else."

"Sounds like magic is involved."

"Yes. It explains why these would-be killers are so bad at what they do. They've probably never killed anyone before and don't even want to do it."

"Let's be thankful they're bad at their job."

"And let's hope they don't get better at it."

It was time for me to go. I'd totally neglected my work at the inn, though I could honestly say it wasn't my fault.

"Feel better and stay safe," I said, touching her hand. "And if you get any relevant premonitions, call me right away."

"I promise I will."

As soon as Room 303 was no longer a crime scene, I went inside to assess how much work it needed. The Simpsons had filled the dresser with clothes, while more garments hung in the closet. Their toilet articles spread over the small vanity table beside the bathroom pedestal sink. A towel still lay on the floor, and the empty champagne bottle sat in the trash can with used tissues and other detritus of life.

Usually, housekeepers turn over a room when it has been

emptied of all the traces of the previous guest, except their trash and perhaps a forgotten possession. When they clean a room still occupied, the housekeeper only makes up the bed, vacuums, cleans the bathroom, and replaces towels. The room is occupied, lived in, with the presence of the guest, out and about doing touristy things, lingering like a ghost.

Here, in 303, the room had to be turned over, but it still contained the presence and possessions of the Simpsons.

And it had an actual ghost lingering.

I sat in one of the two easy chairs and thought about the ghost. Did it affect her that another person, besides her, fell to his death from the very same window she was pushed from? I didn't know why I was curious about that.

"Hello?" I said aloud. "Are you here, Helga?"

She didn't answer, of course. But I sensed her. When you have paranormal abilities, it makes you extra sensitive to psychic energy and the supernatural. I lacked the ability to contact spirits directly. I wasn't a medium like Gloria. But I did have a connection with spirits that normal people, their minds focused on the mundane, do not.

"I know about your sorrow," I said. "I'm here for you if you need me. You're welcome in my inn."

The words flowed from me unplanned. I didn't come to this room intending to make friends with a ghost. My purpose was planning how to put the room back to normal. That included erasing the trauma in the psychic energies.

And that included making sure the resident ghost was okay.

A drawer opened slightly in the bedside table closest to me. I was startled, but happy. She was responding to me.

"The bad energy will go away soon," I said. "We'll make sure your room is peaceful again. I only wish you would find peace, yourself."

The drawer closed.

I sat quietly for a while. But, sure enough, here in the world of the living, my giant to-do list and piles of worries poked through the bubble of my mindfulness. I would need to go downstairs soon.

Then I caught movement in the corner of my eye. I turned my head and got a glimpse of a young woman with red hair, in a dress with a high collar and a hem that covered her ankles.

As I turned my eyes to her, she was gone.

"It was nice meeting you," I said.

AFTER I SERVED TEA, I CALLED MOM.

"So how is Sophie doing, really?" I asked.

"She's fine," Mom said. "You just saw her for yourself."

"I know, but I don't trust my instincts now. I've been going through some strange stuff lately."

"What do you mean?"

"Never mind. I don't want to involve my family. I don't want to put you at risk."

"Now you've got me worried. Is this about the Memory Guild?"

"Yeah."

"Ever since you've been involved with them, you've been exposed to danger. I thought they only preserved the past."

"They preserve truth. And this is not their fault."

"You won't tell me what's going on?"

"It's nothing to be concerned about."

"If you wish to be that way."

Mom knew I was lying. Mothers develop that instinct before

their children are even old enough to lie. Which brought me back to the original topic.

"Has Sophie asked you for more money?"

"A little bit, here and there," Mom said.

"Does she pay you back?"

"With her time, helping me out in the store. You know, if you spoke with her more often, you wouldn't have to ask me about her."

"I told you why I haven't invited her to the inn recently. Because people are turning up dead there. But she could call me more often, too. It seems like the only times I hear from her are when she needs money. And if I turn her down, she calls me less often. Sophie is twenty-four. I try not to smother her."

"She said she's taken on an extra shift at the restaurant, so that's being responsible."

"Yes, it is." I had a dark thought. "Has she been wearing the antique watch you gave her for her birthday?"

A long pause.

"Not lately. But, you know, everyone wears only smart watches nowadays."

"I wouldn't be surprised if she pawned it. Keep an eye out for it."

"Do you think she's been buying drugs?"

"That's what I'm worried about."

"She has seemed preoccupied lately. And she's rarely here. But she's never seemed like she's on something."

"Good. Thanks, Mom. I'll stop interrogating you."

I felt guilty being Suspicious Mom. Sophie was a grown woman, responsible for her own wellbeing. But Sophie's rocky history with drugs will always haunt me with guilt that somehow I was to blame, that I hadn't prevented it, and hadn't seen the signs early enough. Guilt led to tens of thousands spent putting her in recovery programs. And, still, she dropped out and ended up with the sleazy operation that gave her to the vampires.

I couldn't let her get into trouble again and risk ending up in jail or overdosing. But I had to be very careful handling this. I didn't want her believing I assumed the worst about her. But, then again, I always hoped for the best.

CHAPTER 11

VAMPIRES CAN HACK IT

Diego Fernandez lived in an apartment above a restaurant on the fringes of Old Town. He owned the building and the restaurant, which combined traditional Spanish cuisine with American soul food. I hadn't been there yet, but it was said that Diego was a convivial host, hanging out in the bar every evening and greeting all his guests by name. He had a reputation over the years of never appearing to grow older, which, his patrons didn't realize, was because he was a vampire. His restaurant was, no surprise, not open for lunch.

Archibald had arranged my meeting with Diego. I asked Archibald to invite him to my inn, but the gargoyle said a vampire couldn't enter another vampire's home without an invitation from the vampire. Even though the building's deed was in my name, Roderick still laid claim to the property in his deluded mind. And he didn't want to invite Diego.

I arrived at the restaurant, 14 Granada Street, around 7:30 p.m. after the inn's exterior doors were locked and accessible only by guests. The building was two stories and made of brick with wooden hurricane shutters. It looked to have been built during the Civil War era. Diego greeted me warmly at the door.

"Welcome, my friend," he said with a smile. He wore a black turtleneck and had a gold hoop earring in his left ear that looked like one a pirate would wear. "Come sit with me."

He led me into the bar area in a room off the dining area, past a small crowd at the bar, to a table for two by the window.

"Gus," he said to the bartender in his Old-Country Spanish accent. "Two glasses of Albariño, please."

"I didn't know vampires drank wine," I said.

"For the sensory pleasures. Not for intoxication, alas."

The bartender dropped off the glasses of white wine. The amber, medium-bodied wine was crisp, with hints of grapefruit.

"Thank you for agreeing to meet with me," I said.

"But of course. You are a fellow Guild member. And Archibald said you have a plan."

"Not a very clever one, though. I think we should stake out Lance Mewling's home and follow him everywhere. If we're lucky, we'll find evidence that he's behind the assassination plots. But more likely, we might find proof that he's having an affair, and we can use that as leverage to force him to call off the plots."

I explained about The Truth Squad and his army of fanatical supporters.

"Hmm. Not the most elegant plan." He rested his chin in his hand. He had a neatly trimmed goatee. "But I have nothing better to suggest."

"If you could devote your nights after your restaurant closes to surveilling him, I can share the other hours with Guild members."

"Yes, I will. But why aren't the police doing this?"

"Because he denied any knowledge of the plot, and the police don't have any reason to suspect him."

"It is a bit of a stretch to believe he would murder several people peripherally involved in getting him fired."

"The assassins fit the profile of his followers," I said. "They're amateurs. Enthusiastic, but untrained. If I can find a way to hack into their secret message board, that would go a long way. Why doesn't the Guild have a computer hacker?"

Diego laughed.

"Because hacking doesn't require supernatural abilities. When we need to do computer forensics work, we hire it out. But I'm not so bad with coding, myself."

"You? You're like five hundred years old. My mother is only in her late seventies and can't figure out how to turn a computer on."

"Oh, please," Diego said with a smile. "I'm only thirty-eight in body age—the age I was when I was turned. My brain is quite nimble. Since the early days, when I was a master at navigating with a sextant, I've kept up with all the constantly evolving technology. Give me a link to the message board, and I'll see what I can do."

"And there's something else," I said. "A supernatural element. The first assassin who was assigned to me, who was herself murdered in my inn, was killed in a manner that suggested a non-human entity."

"That's what I heard."

"And I read the memories of the assassin who attacked James. There seemed to be an external force influencing his thoughts. Maybe something supernatural."

"Interesting. Perhaps, there is more to this story than getting revenge for losing a job."

"My thoughts exactly," I said, downing the rest of my wine.

Diego glanced at his watch. "I think I'll try to crack that message board now. You don't have to stick around, but I'd like to get moving on this. I'm one of the few Guild members who hasn't been attacked yet."

"Let's do it," I said.

Diego left the table and returned with his laptop and a fresh glass of Albariño for me.

He pushed the laptop, with an open browser window, toward me.

"Show me the path you took before you were blocked."

I didn't remember exactly how I got there last time. So I scrolled through comments on Mewling's website until I found one that had a link to a thread on the 8kun site. Once there, I dug deeper, finding a reference to The Truth Squad. Clicking on more links, I eventually ended up on a page that said "Access Denied. Password Required." I pushed the laptop back to Diego.

"Ah, I see. Pretty standard stuff," he said. "I'm going to try a Dictionary Attack. Nothing clever. It's a brute-force automation that rapidly generates passwords in popular combinations of phrases, letters, numbers, and symbols until it eventually lands on the correct one."

He opened an application I didn't recognize and typed several lines of code. Finally, he leaned back in his chair.

"Nothing to do now, but wait."

"How long does it take?"

"Sometimes, mere minutes. But if the passwords are complex, it could take hours."

I took a long sip of wine.

"I thought I'd be working with long-ago history for the Guild," I said. "Not this."

"Everything in the present moment has connections to history. That's the nature of time."

Suddenly, he stiffened. He frowned and canted his head to one side.

"What is it?" I asked.

"I hear something. In the alley behind the kitchen."

I, of course, heard nothing except the low music and hum of conversation in the room. But I wasn't a vampire.

He stood and looked like he was about to sprint through the restaurant to the back door, but held himself back. His customers wouldn't know he was a vampire, and rocketing through the space at preternatural speed wasn't a good idea. Instead, he quickly went out the front entrance. I caught a motion-blur of a figure racing around to the side of the building. I went outside after him.

He was long gone, but I went down the alley between his house and a similar one next door.

A muffled scream came from behind the building. I ran faster.

Behind the house was a small parking lot, a dumpster, and a spot for delivery trucks to back up to the kitchen's outside door. I couldn't see anyone at first. Then, a body flew over my head and landed in the dumpster.

Diego emerged from the shadows behind the house into the porch light. He held what looked like a pile of modeling clay with wires hanging from it.

"The low-life was planting a bomb," he said.

"Can bombs kill vampires?" I asked.

"Yes. Sometimes. And it could have killed anyone else in the building, and maybe people next door or passing by. Not to mention, destroying a historic building and a very successful business. They picked the wrong guy to mess with."

Remember, you don't want to make a vampire angry.

Diego walked to the dumpster. It was half full, so the bomber was easy to reach. Diego grabbed him by the seat of his pants and yanked him out, dropping him on the ground in front of us. The man was still conscious, more frightened than injured. Diego could have killed him as easily as squashing a bug.

"Who hired you?" the vampire asked.

The man only moaned in reply.

Diego reached down and grabbed him by the throat with one hand. He lifted the man, holding him with his feet dangling a foot above the parking lot.

"Answer me."

"No one hired me," the man said, gasping for breath. "I answered the call. I'm a patriot."

"You're a coward," Diego said. "What call did you answer?"

"To join The Truth Squad. To punish His enemies."

The man was frightened, but bold in his convictions. He was a scrawny guy with long hair and the word "truth" tattooed on his forehead.

It was ironic that I belonged to a guild devoted to preserving actual, historic truth. And here we were fighting a bunch of deranged people who claimed to follow the cause of truth, though one that was completely divorced from reality.

"Punish whose enemies?" Diego demanded.

"The Great One's. The one chosen by God."

"Be a little more specific. Plenty of lunatics claim to be chosen by God."

"Lance Mewling. The greatest patriot our country has ever known."

I knew it!

"Lance Mewling ordered you to plant this bomb?" I asked.

"No, no, no," the man said. He smiled, clearly feeling smarter than us. Even though he was being held by his throat a foot above the ground. "The Great One doesn't concern himself with puny people like me."

"You're right about being puny," Diego said. "Who, exactly, ordered you to do this?"

"No one. Everyone. The voices tell me. The voices command me. I obey the Word." His eyes rolled backwards until only the whites were showing. He laughed and babbled incoherently.

A chill ran through my scalp. This guy was acting like he was possessed. In the beginning, he had seemed cogent. Not anymore.

Diego groaned in frustration and tossed the man back into the dumpster twenty feet away.

"The police will have to deal with him," he said, making a call on his phone. He reported the attempted bombing and the capture of the suspect.

We guarded the man in the dumpster until the police arrived. Diego spoke to a detective I didn't recognize. He reported that the bomber had mentioned Lance Mewling. After what seemed like an eternity, the interviews were done, and we returned to the restaurant. It was empty, except for the staff closing up.

"I wish it was as simple as Mewling ordering these hits, but it's not," I said.

"He could be, through choosing mentally ill followers."

"But didn't you sense the presence of the supernatural?"

"Yeah. You're right," Diego said as he sat down at his laptop on the table where he had left it. "Well, we got in."

He turned the screen toward me. It looked like any internet forum, with several topics followed by strings of comments.

I sat down and scrolled through the topics. They were violent and unsettling. This forum, a subset of others started by the followers of Lance Mewling, was all about seeking retribution. Public figures who allegedly committed transgressions against Mewling were named, and people described in gleeful detail how they wanted to harm these figures.

Many of the threads were about The Truth Squad. The posters had obviously heard about it, but knew very little. So, the posts were questions about the squad, along with lots of speculation. Being a member of The Truth Squad was treated as the most glorious honor a person could earn.

But no one knew how to join it. There were plenty of rumors and guesswork. But no one had a definitive answer.

The only thing they all agreed on was that you didn't ask to join The Truth Squad. The Truth Squad asked you.

Only when "The Word" came to you, would you be chosen. Then you must obey "The Word."

No one knew who gave this word. Some thought it came from Lance Mewling, though most believed it came from a higher source, from God himself.

Or someone or something they thought was God.

"I feel like I've learned so much," I said. "But I've learned nothing helpful."

"I'll continue to monitor the activity on this board. But all we can do for now is proceed with your original plan."

An old-fashioned stake out.

LANCE MEWLING LIVED IN A MULTI-MILLION-DOLLAR MANSION on the beach. Good for him. Also, good for me. You see, an equivalently priced home out in the country would be walled in on several acres of land, perhaps too far from the gate for passersby to even see it. Mewling's home was right there on a slight crest beside the coastal road, A1A. Sure, there was a gate at the end of his driveway, but his driveway was only a few dozen yards long. I easily found a place to park across the street near some condos, and could observe anyone coming or going from his house. With binoculars, I could probably get an excellent view of their faces.

And as much as the rich people hate it, there was nothing keeping me from walking along the beach and checking out the oceanfront exposure of his house.

So I sat there across the street all day, except when I had to slip back to the inn to perform my duties. I didn't see Mewling leave at all. I was pretty sure he was at home, based on all the giant black SUVs parked in the driveway and the constant activity of the household staff.

He didn't get any visitors, either, unless you counted package delivery vans as visitors.

I asked Julie to serve afternoon tea for me, so I was there all afternoon long. Finally, bored out of my mind, I drove to the nearby beach access, parked, and walked along the sand to Mewling's home. The tide was out, so there was plenty of fine, hard-packed sand to make for easy walking.

I realized I hadn't been on the beach for a while. A large flock of terns clustered at the edge of the receding surf, and a line of pelicans glided just above the dunes. The sky was clear blue, and the sun wasn't yet below the roofs of Mewling and his wealthy neighbors. I savored the salt in the air and the mild southeast breeze.

If I had an oceanfront mansion, and I was someone people believed was anointed by God, you'd better believe I'd be outside enjoying a day like this.

And sure enough, I thought I spotted him. The fat guy on the lounge chair by the giant swimming pool. He wore shorts and a short-sleeved shirt that was pushed up by his belly. He stared at a tablet, probably watching videos of himself.

I hadn't carried my binoculars because it would have been too obvious to be staring through them at a house from the beach. So I drifted up the sand dunes dangerously close to the house to get a better look.

I wasn't the kind of woman who attracted a lot of attention. I wasn't a hot young thing in a bikini. Or someone who had no business wearing a bikini. People like that get noticed, too. I was a petite woman in midlife in a wide-brimmed hat, T-shirt, and shorts. From a distance, I probably looked like a harmless old lady. Perhaps, my anonymity made me too confident as I wandered through the sea oats at the top of the dune. Only some prickly pear cacti and a patch of lawn separated me from the swimming pool.

"Can I help you?"

I almost jumped out of my sandals at the man's voice behind me.

He didn't wear a uniform, just a white polo shirt and khakis. But I was pretty sure he was a security guard, the way he studied me through his dark shades. And it wasn't the way a woman liked to be studied: like a potential threat.

I played dumb.

"Is this Lance Mewling's house?" I asked in an exaggerated Southern accent. "I heard he lives around here."

"Sorry, ma'am, but you're on private property here. Please get back on the beach."

"That's him, isn't it? Oh, please let me get an autograph."

"Sorry, ma'am, he doesn't like to be disturbed. I have to ask you to leave since you're trespassing."

"Oh, just a little autograph wouldn't hurt anyone. I'm such a huge fan of his."

"I hate to disappoint a fan."

It was God's messenger himself. He had wandered over to the patch of lawn on this side of the pool.

I pulled a pen from my purse and the only paper I could find, a shipping invoice for toilet tissue. The security guard allowed me to hand them to the Great Man.

"Please make it out to the Memory Guild," I said.

Mewling grunted in affirmation as he signed the folded paper. He had once been a handsome man, at least with TV makeup, but he looked old and dissolute to me. His nose had turned into a cauliflower drinker's nose.

He returned the paper and pen to me. I thanked him profusely and hurried across the dune and onto the beach.

All the way, I clutched the paper and pen and tried to pick up his thoughts. The best I could read was: *The Memory Guild? That's a weird name for a club.*

He hadn't heard of us. So why was he trying to kill us?

Maybe he held the pen and paper for too short of a time, and his mind was elsewhere. But if anything would trigger an emotional response from him, I figured it would be the name of the Guild. And it didn't.

There was no way I knew of that Gloria, James, and I would be connected to Dr. Noordlun other than through the Guild. Again, I understood why Mewling would hate the professor, the face of the public opposition against him. But why us? Why little old me?

The sun had dipped behind the row of mansions, putting much of the beach in shadow. After dark fell, Diego would be here watching the house. With his vampire senses, he could catch anything going on.

And night was when the bad stuff happens.

CHAPTER 12

THE THINGS THEY LEFT BEHIND

I returned to the inn in time to put out the wine and cheese. We were back up to a whopping thirty-six percent capacity, with a fourth room booked. It was a young couple with big-city airs. They polished off an entire bottle of Cabernet in the parlor, while the other guests showed more restraint, but they didn't mingle much.

"I'm headed home now," Julie said. "Need to cook dinner for Frank."

Frank was her brother, who had suffered a mild stroke at the age of sixty, forcing an early retirement. He was one of the reasons Julie had gone back to work and taken the job at the inn, which, let's face it, was menial for someone of her education.

"Okay. Thanks, Julie, for covering for me today."

"What were you up to? Looks like you got a lot of sun."

"Oh, I was playing private detective."

"How so? C'mon, your secret is safe with me."

I knew I should keep my mouth shut, but the glass of sherry I'd just downed didn't help. Julie knew about the gunman's attack on me the other day, but not the rest of it. I filled her in on Monique Simpson's intentions, though I didn't explain how I knew. I mentioned the attempts on the lives of my "friends," as well as the injuries of Gloria.

"Wow," Julie said. "Aren't the police doing anything?"

"There's usually an officer parked across the street from here, but, no, they don't seem to be investigating much. So I have this theory that there's a rich man who wants revenge on Dr. Noordlun and anyone who helped in getting this man fired."

"Who is the rich man?" Julie asked.

"Oh, I shouldn't say."

"You have to, now. Don't leave me hanging."

"He used to be a local television celebrity. And now, he's big on the internet."

Julie furrowed her brow in concentration.

"Lance Mewling?" she asked.

I said nothing, but gave a knowing smile.

"Oh, that pig." She snorted in disgust. "Be careful."

"I will. I'm really just keeping my mind occupied, so I don't go crazy while the police hopefully solve this. Thanks for your extra hours in covering for me."

"It's my pleasure," she said with a smile. "Stay safe, Darla."

Shortly after Julie left, I received an email notification from my reservation service that another room had been booked for next week. It cheered me up, until I realized it was Room 303. It was clean now, and had been listed as available, but I still needed to clear out the few remaining possessions Monique had left up there when she moved to 201 in the futile attempt to get a more restful sleep.

I cleaned up after the wine and cheese, then headed to my cottage for a quick dinner. Afterwards, I decided to get room 303 over with. In case I needed it, I grabbed an empty box from the inn's storeroom and rode the rickety elevator to the third floor and the haunted room.

I forgot to cover my hand before touching the doorknob, and the memory from nearly a century and a half ago filled my mind: paranoid anger at a new bride—

—and how could she do this to me on our honeymoon? The tour operator with his sleazy smile. He was looking at me with contempt, knowing I was a cuckold, while she giggled and flirted. I shouldn't have lost control and confronted her. Her look of astonishment at my accusation made me regret it and doubt myself, but now the rage and uncertainty have returned. And there she sits on the windowsill, looking all innocent, while she is probably waiting for his carriage to go by. Fear crosses her face as she sees my anger. How could she do this on our honeymoon of all times? I move toward—

—I yanked my hand away. I'd experienced this memory before, of the first person to be pushed from this window before Dennis Simpson's recent fatal fall. I didn't want to go through that experience again.

"Helga? Are you here?" I said aloud to the ghost.

She didn't show herself this time. My previous encounter with her didn't cause me any fear. All I felt was her bafflement at her unexpected death. I was certain she had been innocent of her husband's paranoid delusions. I had read that the court had declared him mentally ill and instead of being hanged, he had rotted away in whatever form of asylum we had back in those days. Two lives destroyed for naught.

I hoped to encounter Helga's ghost again. Maybe, I could impart to her soul some form of comfort.

In the meantime, I had work to do. I opened the closet. One suitcase sat on the floor, presumably Dennis'. He had three shirts, two pairs of trousers, and a sport coat hanging. I folded them carefully and placed them in the suitcase. I wanted them to look presentable to whatever relative received the shipped suitcase.

I opened the drawers of the dresser against the wall opposite the bed. The top two were empty. The bottom two held more of his clothing: underwear, socks, T-shirts, and a pair of shorts.

When I removed the last item, the shorts, I found a shallow leather case hidden beneath them. The leather was ancient with minute cracks. The top of the case was a flap held closed by brass snaps. As my hand neared it, a flare of hot energy burned my fingertips, and I yanked my hand back.

There were some serious memories in this thing, and I didn't have time or energy to read them now. I shielded my hands with a pair of socks like oven pads, picked up the case, and placed it atop the folded clothes in the suitcase.

Curiosity overcame me. I simply had to see what was inside. Still protected by the socks, I pulled the flap, feeling the brass button-fasteners pop free.

The velvet-lined case was empty. In the center was a sunken velvet-lined cavity in the shape of the item it was meant to hold:

A long dagger with a cross-guard.

It had to be the ancient, jewel-encrusted dagger Detective Leper found beneath the bed in 201, where Monique had been cut open.

I turned the case over and examined the bottom. The leather was slightly more cracked on this side. There were no adornments, but at the bottom right were three tiny words in gold lettering. I squinted to see them better.

Flores-Mirada, Toledo

Toledo was a city in Spain once famous for sword-making. The name must be the dagger's owner or its maker. I put down the socks and took a picture of the writing with my phone.

Why was the case hidden among her husband's things? Did

the dagger belong to him rather than her? Why did he bring it on their vacation? How did whoever killed her know about it, and why was it used?

I was full of questions, wasn't I?

Also, I thought the police had searched this room. Why hadn't they found it? Maybe because it would have meant nothing to the officer searching the room after an accidental falling death. Monique wasn't murdered until the following morning, in a different room, and only then was the dagger found. That room was undoubtedly searched more thoroughly before being sealed off.

I would have to give this empty leather case to the police. After I read it, of course. And that would happen when I was calm and steady, without the nervous stomach I had right now.

I checked the room, and there was nothing left of the Simpsons here. Hopefully, neither of them would come back as ghosts to compete with Helga for haunting rights. The bedroom and bathroom were already clean and would be ready for guests.

I brought the suitcase downstairs and put it in the storage room until we found a relative who wanted us to ship it. I removed the leather case, however, and brought it to my cottage. This time, I used actual oven mitts to avoid touching it with my skin. Through the thick mitts, I felt power pulsing.

I prepared for bed, but kept glancing at the case sitting on my dresser. No one was going to tell me the results of the forensics tests on the knife, but when I read Lepore's thoughts, she was convinced it had been the murder weapon.

But so many other questions nagged me. Had Monique been killed by her fellow assassins to punish her for not completing her assignment? If so, how did they know about the knife and where it was hidden? The squad seemed too incompetent to have pulled off such a gruesome yet mess-free murder. Then again, they stupidly left the murder weapon behind.

And what role did the supernatural play? I was convinced an unearthly power was involved somehow. I could sense it right there in the leather case. But was it a human using magic, or did a spirit entity kill Monique?

The case might have my answers. It wouldn't hold memories of Monique's death; those would be on the dagger which hadn't been returned to the case. But it would hold the thoughts and intentions of whoever opened the case and removed the knife. And it would have memories of previous things the weapon had been used for, whether they were murders or cleaning someone's fingernails.

The case lay on my dresser like a hot young stud trying to entice me.

The sensible side of me was rapidly losing ground to the impatient, curious side.

I could afford to stay up a little later, right?

I approached the dresser, drank in the scent of the old leather of the case, of strange oils used to preserve it and to protect the steel blade kept inside. Centuries of dust particles from exotic places. Perhaps that coppery scent was traces of blood left behind from a blade not properly cleaned after a killing.

The leather case, simple and unadorned, was seducing me, not just with its scent and my lust to touch it, but with the secrets it kept from me.

I did it. I touched rich, smooth leather with my bare hands. And I—

—should bring a weapon with me to the other room. That sense of something watching me makes me feel unsafe. It's not a person. And it's not the ghost of the newlywed. Dennis would be furious with me for

opening this case. I think he believed I didn't know he had it. He likes to play morally superior to me because I'm supposed to kill someone, but he traffics in artifacts from heists. He's no angel. I just don't know why he wanted to keep this dagger. (Unsnap the flap and hold it open.) Yes, the dagger is magnificent, with the diamonds and sapphires inset in the cross-guard and pommel, and the handle wrapped with gold wire. The steel is magnificent, only slightly pitted with rust. The edges are sharp. This is a good killing weapon. But why am I so reluctant to touch it? There are some bad vibes here, just like that feeling I have of being watched. But I need to get over it and take this knife. I need a weapon.

Before the police came to my room, I had to hide the gun I was going to use on Chesswick, so I put it on the top of the stairs to the attic. But I can't find the attic door now. I swear it was right down the hall from our room. Yet I can't find it. I must be going crazy. It doesn't matter. I don't have time now to look for that stupid door. I just want to sleep, and I can't do it in this room. The dagger will be enough to make me feel safer. But wow, the handle feels warm—hot, almost. This is one creepy dagger. Come on, you lethal thing, let's go—

—and that was the end of the vision. I let go of the case. She must have released it, too, at the point her memory ended.

It was interesting that she was afraid of something watching her, but not a person. She wasn't worried about The Truth Squad coming after her.

But what struck me the most about her memory was the mention of the attic that didn't exist. And the door that appeared and disappeared randomly.

The door, I was certain, led to the In Between. The plane of existence between worlds and between the living and the dead.

The place I suspected Cory had disappeared to by accident, when I had believed he walked out on me.

Now, there was a gun in the In Between. I wondered if Cory needed one.

But, back to the task at hand. I wouldn't get any more memories from the leather case of the night Monique was murdered. But I sensed the case held many memories of many people over the years. Did I dare sample them?

There were plenty of memories just on the outside of the case that I would dig into at some point before I gave it to the police. I was more curious about what the inside held, especially in the velvet-lined cavity that would hold the dagger in place.

I took a deep breath and reached with my index finger into the cavity—

—the brutal moaning of emptiness, the vicious whining of petulance, the hunger to destroy all who stand against you, the perverted desire to defile all that is sacred, the urge to hurt, to maim, to damage, to kill, to—

—I yanked my hand back. No, no, no, I would not experience this crap. Not tonight, at least. There was too much evil and dark desire in here. Perhaps, some sense can be made of it, but I didn't have the strength to deal with it now.

One thing I knew for sure: There was serious evil associated with that dagger, in the weapon itself, or in the souls of those who had wielded it. Or in the entity that controlled it.

I wanted this leather case far, far from my inn. But I knew it held clues. For solving what, I hadn't a clue.

CHAPTER 13

READING MEMORIES

The internet had little to say about Flores-Mirada of Toledo. Which wasn't surprising, since the name belonged to a family of armorers, who made custom swords and daggers for the wealthy of Spain in the sixteen hundreds. I found this out from websites of auction houses that sold two of the rare weapons, as well as from an article in a magazine for collectors. Of course, I didn't find any mention of the specific dagger in question.

Then, I did some general searches for "Spanish dagger inlaid jewels," in some cases including "seventeenth century." The results were very random and not illuminating. Until one caught my eye.

It was a news article about a treasure museum being burglarized. It happened to belong to Jules Monsignor, the treasure hunter, who was one of the people The Memory Guild had clashed with after he destroyed the remains of a shipwreck. The museum had the completely unimaginative name of Jules Monsignor's Treasure Museum. It appeared to be more of a tourist attraction than a scholarly historical institution.

The article mentioned that the thieves took more than gold doubloons and silver pieces-of-eight. They also stole personal items, jewelry, and weaponry found in shipwrecks, and treasure found on land. The article mentioned a string of rare pearls, an unusual golden tool for removing ear wax, and a dagger inlaid with jewels.

Was this the same dagger? I was determined to find out.

Next, I went to the treasure museum's website and social media feeds, where I browsed through photos of its treasure collection. I found three images that showed the dagger fairly well, one of which allowed me to zoom in for a detailed look.

The only image I had of Dennis Simpson's dagger was from the memory of it Monique left on the leather case as she looked at the dagger.

It was the same dagger; I was certain of it. The museum photo even included the leather case propped up behind the dagger in their display.

The museum website mentioned the dagger was found on land, in a hidden crypt below the ruins of an early colonial building in San Marcos. The crypt was referred to as the "Spanish Inquisition Chamber," because crucifixes and other religious items were also found there, along with torture devices.

Yes, torture.

There were thumbscrews, a Judas cradle, and other unspecified devices.

I hadn't known the Spanish Inquisition stretched as far as San Marcos. The religious body that claimed to fight heresy, while usually harming innocent people, was said to have operated in the colonial territories of Mexico and Peru at its height. San Marcos was basically a backwater garrison town at the time.

It didn't seem like the kind of place to attract the prosecutors of the Inquisition. Maybe the museum was playing loose with history to make these items more notorious.

Aside from doing unpaid work for Detective Lepore, what did my identifying the dagger mean? That I had much more work to do. I wanted to find out why Dennis Simpson had the dagger, and whether he was involved in the burglary of the museum. Was there significance in this weapon being used to kill his wife? And did someone from The Truth Squad kill her? If not, then who?

Finally, I wanted to know the source of the ominous supernatural presence I sensed in the dagger's case and that Monique had felt bearing down on her the night she died.

I reminded myself that these questions were merely my personal curiosity. My main concern should be trying to stop The Truth Squad from killing me and my fellow Guild members. But still, the dagger was used to kill a guest in my inn, and I needed to know if it had brought evil with it to my property.

The first step would be to delve more deeply into the memories attached to the dagger's case. And I needed help from a more experienced psychometrist. That would be Laurel from the Guild.

After another day of sitting in my car across the street from Mewling's mansion, hoping for some action with his extramarital activities, I drove to Laurel's home.

Laurel lived at the beach, but in completely different circumstances than Mewling. Her home was far from being a mansion. It was a 1930s-era bungalow in a neighborhood down the Sangre River from San Marcos. Her home, half a block from the beach, was built high off the ground with a wrap-around porch, and was covered with cypress shingles. It had survived hurricanes, nor'easters, and developers, with charm and quaintness. This was my first time here.

"Welcome!" she called to me in her Southern accent as I climbed the old wooden steps to the porch. She waited at the top in her wheelchair.

"What a lovely home," I said. "And such a perfect location."

"I don't get out on the beach much, and only with my chair that has the big tires. I call it my dune buggy. But see, if I'm in this corner of the porch, I get a nice view down the street of the ocean."

I went and stood beside her. She was right. It was a magnificent view. There were only two homes between her and the beach.

Laurel looked at the tote bag I carried.

"Looks like you brought our patient."

"I also wrapped it in cloth for handling," I said.

"Oh boy. It's that strong?"

"To me, it is. Remember, I'm a beginner at this."

"But you could identify what you felt as evil."

"Yeah, like an aching in my bones. Not to mention, the chills going up my spine. I wonder if that wasn't my psychometry, but was some vestigial sense inherited from early humans."

"Paranormal abilities like ours are inherited, too," she said. "Although, we need to learn how to control and strengthen them."

"I've improved my ability already with what you've taught me. But I still have a long way to go, as I learned with this dagger case. It wasn't that I was frightened; I couldn't process the psychic energy. It was too strong. It was like trying to drink from a firehose instead of a straw."

"Yes, it can be dangerous if your mind is too sympathetic,

and you read memories that are too powerful. Or too evil. The Guild lost a psychometrist that way once before."

Laurel's pretty, but placid, face showed a sudden pinch of anxiety.

"We don't have to do this," I said. "It's something that intrigues me, but it probably has nothing to do with the threats we're facing now."

"Reading memories is what I do," Laurel said. "Not just for the Guild, but as my contribution to history. Now, let's go inside to my study."

She led the way inside, through a sunroom and down a short hallway to a small, square room, empty except for a chair and a small table in front of it. The room had no windows, just the one doorway and four walls painted white. A single light fixture hung from the middle of the ceiling.

"There is nothing to distract in here," Laurel said. "I find the bare white walls help when I have visions and my eyes are open. They're almost like a movie screen."

Laurel directed me to close the door, and sit on the chair while she positioned her wheelchair across the small table from me. The inside of the door was white as well, making the room feel like a sensory deprivation chamber.

"The exterior of the case contains memories of those who have handled it," I said, "though I've only read the most recent person, the guest at my inn. Inside is where the real power lies, residues of the memories on the dagger."

I tipped the tote bag, allowing the leather case, wrapped in fabric, to slide out onto the table. I put on gloves and unwrapped the fabric, revealing the leather case.

"I will touch the case," Laurel said. "You will touch my hands, being very careful not to touch the case. I will bear the brunt of the psychic energy, while you will experience a watered-down version of what I feel."

"Will I be receiving input that's been filtered through your mind?" I asked.

"No, there will be none of my subjective interpretation. You'll receive input from the object, filtered through my senses. It's necessary to protect you at your level of skill."

"I understand."

"Okay, then let us proceed," Laurel said, placing both palms on the cover of the case without the least bit of hesitation.

Watching her face, I put my hands, also palms down, upon hers. They were larger than mine and muscular, from years of pushing wheelchair wheels.

At first, I felt nothing, except for the gradual warming of her hands.

Then dozens of voices broke out in my head, all speaking at the same time in a cacophony. My view of Laurel's face, calm, eyes staring at the wall behind me, dissolved to a kaleidoscope of images of faces and rooms and of the leather case itself, as viewed through the eyes of all those who had handled it.

I was confused and disoriented. It was as if I was holding on to Laurel during an amusement park ride.

"Relax," she said. "This is my method. You can't use this gift passively. You must always be in control. What I'm doing is taking in the totality of memories contained here, from a high angle. Then, if we wish, we can zoom into certain memories, so to speak. Do you see any that are relevant?

I didn't. They were all unfamiliar and meaningless to me.

Until I saw the interior of Room 303. Not through Monique's eyes, but through Dennis' as he placed the leather case in the dresser drawer and covered it with shirts.

I didn't even have to tell Laurel; she knew this memory interested me because our consciousnesses were now entwined. Together, we dove into the memory—

—Of my love for the dagger, my happiness that I had acquired it. My lust for its power. My distrust of Monique and her bunch of amateur-hour buffoons that called themselves The Truth Squad. A bunch of unprofessional losers who were just cultists in my opinion—

—why did he have the dagger? What was his intent? We plunged deeper, back in time, to when Dennis initially packed the case in his suitcase in their home in Georgia—

—wheeling the suitcase into the cold garage at night while Monique is asleep, removing the leather case from its hiding spot beneath the workbench, placing it in the suitcase, random images of palm trees and the skyline of San Marcos and a French restaurant three blocks from the inn and then, out of nowhere, images of the cathedral's exterior on the City Square, and images of the rows of pews and the altar up ahead and then of the confessional booths, the thick smell of incense, and then the excitement grows and my heart beats like a jackhammer . . . and then the suitcase zippered shut—

—Laurel's hands were warmer now, I thought, as she removed them from the case when we snapped out of it as Dennis' memory ended.

"Interesting," I said. "I wish we could have learned more what his intentions were."

"I fear that's the best we can get. I sense very little energy of his prior to that. I don't think he handled the case much before that memory. There was definitely the sense he was trying to keep it hidden as much as possible. He must have had many thoughts about acquiring it in the first place, but that actual act was probably just grabbing it, or having it handed to him, and sticking it in a bag."

"Yeah. And there wasn't much energy on his suitcase when I packed it yesterday," I said.

"How did they get from Georgia to San Marcos? Did they fly or drive?"

"I think they drove. Wow, I totally forgot about their car. I figured the police would have impounded it. Since we have so little parking at the inn, if guests park in a city lot we reimburse them."

"I bet there are a lot of memories in the car during their drive here, thinking of their plans."

"Absolutely. I have to find that car."

"Well, are you ready to dive into the heavy stuff?" Laurel asked, studying my face.

"Yeah," I took a deep breath. "It's going to be harder on you."

"And on you. This time, you can't just go along for the ride. You need to be the safety valve. If we get into some serious poop, and if I can't break the connection, you need to pull my hands away. Got it?"

"Yes." But I was afraid. What if I couldn't break my connection, either?

As if reading my thoughts, Laurel said, "You are insulated by me enough to be able to break away when you want to."

I nodded. We'll see about that.

Laurel unsnapped the case cover and flipped it open without using gloves. Instantly, I had an aching in my bones and goosebumps breaking out on my arms and scalp.

"Wow," Laurel said. "I see what you mean. That knife must have been radioactive with energy to have left so much of it in this case." She looked at me. "Ready?"

I nodded, but she couldn't hide the fear in her eyes. Not very confidence-building. But I placed my hands atop hers as she gently touched the velvet with both index fingers, as if testing if a plate was too hot.

I didn't get any input, which was odd. Laurel moved her fingers closer to the depression shaped like the dagger.

Flickering thoughts and images of Monique grasping the dagger and marveling at how heavy it was—

—*going to be hard defending myself with this if I can barely lift it*—

—then she was gone, and it was just Laurel and me probing the velvet. Where was the jumble of sensory inputs we got from the cover of the case?

I glanced at Laurel, but her eyes were lost in concentration.

Until they opened wide in surprise. Her hands grew feverishly hot. I wondered if—

—*"What are you seeking, little girls? I see you poking around where my dagger belongs. You don't have the slightest idea what you're risking, do you? You really want to experience my thoughts and feelings? Your minds would explode, your eyes would be blinded, your eardrums would burst, your lungs would fill with fire, and your noses would sting from brimstone. You two are tiny, pathetic insects compared to me and my power and knowledge. And I will crush you like the ants you are. You can't begin to imagine the pain of—"*

—being trapped in a dark tunnel with billowing flames and a cloud of sulfurous gas rushing toward us. . .

Laurel's hands were so hot they burned mine as I yanked them away from the leather case.

Her eyes rolled up, and she went into convulsions. I knocked the case from the table, and it clattered upon the floor. Yet Laurel wouldn't come out of her trance. I didn't know what to do.

Somehow, instinct made me grab her wrists and clumsily place her hands on my head and face. I forced myself to think warm, comforting thoughts. Hopefully, they would flow into her, as if I were an inanimate object she was reading.

Then my vision went dark.

I was on my back on the floor. Hardwood, not tile, which had kept my head from splitting open. My chair was lying on its back beside me. I raised my head to look at Laurel, slumped in her wheelchair.

Her chin rested on her chest, and her eyes were closed. My heart clenched at the thought she was dead.

Then she snored, long, ripping snores. And I lay my sore head back upon the floor and smiled.

"It's not human," Laurel said as we sat on her porch and listened to the rumble of the surf. "Maybe it's a demon, though I couldn't say because I've never encountered one before. I didn't believe they really existed, to tell the truth. Sure, I'm all-in with the supernatural, but I thought demons were just metaphors."

"Did you see it?" I asked. We'd been on the porch for twenty minutes, and I'd been waiting for her to bring up what had happened, because I didn't want to ask.

"No, I didn't see it. I saw only darkness until there was fire coming at us. But I felt like the demon was inside my head. Violating me."

"That raises the possibility," I said, "that Monique Simpson was not killed by a human, but by this demon—or whatever it is."

"It did say, '*my* dagger.'"

"Maybe it needs the dagger to be able to kill. Otherwise, we wouldn't be around right now."

"It's interesting that it's clinging to the empty case," Laurel said. "Why isn't it with the dagger?"

"The police have the dagger now. Maybe the demon is in the

evidence room with the dagger, as well as with the case. Who says a demon can't be in two places at once?"

"I think it's time to give the case to the police. We can't get anything else from it. To be honest, I don't want to try."

"Me neither," I said. "We're done with it. But before we write this off, let's brainstorm for a moment. Is there any way the dagger connects with The Truth Squad?"

"I don't see how, other than the fact Mrs. Simpson had access to it. Her husband tried to keep it secret from her."

"But she knew about it and that he had gotten it illicitly. She was thinking that when she opened the case. She didn't just find it in his drawer by accident."

Laurel shrugged.

"Remember," I said, "when I read the handle of the pike the killer tried to use against James, his thoughts suggested he was influenced by some entity."

"Are you saying it's the same entity we just dealt with?"

"It's worth considering. But I can't make sense of the connection."

CHAPTER 14

A VISITOR

"Detective Le-*pore*, I have an item you should have," I said when she approached me at the Police Department's front desk.

"And what would that be, Ms. Chesswick?"

I handed her the tote bag with the cloth-wrapped case inside. The bag said I was an NPR donor, further cementing my virtue.

"When I was packing up the possessions left behind by the Simpsons, I came upon this leather case hidden in a drawer. I believe it belongs to the dagger you found."

She came around the counter and took the bag.

"Thank you," she said with a smile that seemed sincere.

"By the way, I wonder if the dagger is one that was stolen from Jules Monsignor's Treasure Museum."

"Yes, it is," she said, impressed. "We've confirmed that. Looks like you've done some research."

"It would have been nice if you told me you confirmed it."

"Why would it matter to you?"

"I'm not a child. I have an interest in knowing about the murder of my guest in my inn."

"I'm sorry," she said. "I'll keep you better apprised of developments."

I wondered if I should tell her that Dennis was the one who'd acquired the dagger. I didn't feel particularly generous anymore, so I kept quiet. Especially, since I was curious about the supernatural aspects of the dagger, and whether there was a connection between the entity attached to the dagger and The Truth Squad. Speaking of which.

"Have you learned anything more about The Truth Squad?" I asked.

Leper was surprised. "My, you truly have been doing your homework. How did you learn that name?"

"Oh, poking around on the internet."

"Very good," she said. "Where we stand now is, we believe that the attacks have been uncoordinated acts by lone-wolf domestic terrorists who fancy themselves members of this Truth Squad. They worship Lance Mewling, but we have found no evidence that he has communicated with them or ordered their actions, even indirectly. Probably, individuals are spurring them on, but we haven't yet found out who these individuals are."

"Have you found a motive for all this?" I asked.

"Well," she gave a goofy grin, "we think your theory might be partly correct. You and your acquaintances are seen to be enemies of Mewling for some reason, and things just spiraled from there. You have to understand how these conspiracies work. They're all based on false facts, rumors, and misinterpretations. Mix that up with paranoia, and people end up believing all sorts of nutty things. Maybe someone saw an article in which Dr. Noordlun spoke out against Mewling. That gets repeated and distorted through hundreds of mentions on internet forums. Someone searches the internet and finds a Darla Chess associated with Dr. Noordlun. He then searches for her and mistakenly mixes up her name with Darla Chesswick. He asserts you are part of the conspiracy, and this mistake gets repeated so many times, it becomes a fact in their eyes."

"Wow. So, now what? What are my acquaintances and I supposed to do?"

"Nothing, other than be vigilant and careful. We're monitoring the internet forums. There's still a patrol car outside your inn. Call me if you see anything suspicious."

This wasn't reassuring. I thanked her anyway and asked if an officer could keep an eye on Laurel's home, as well. She thanked me for bringing in the dagger case, and I left.

I was skeptical of the lone-wolf theory. The doofuses who attacked us didn't seem capable of taking the initiative to do a hit on their own. Someone was ordering them to do it, whether the supernatural was involved or not. I still believed it was Mewling. The fact he seemed not to recognize the name of The Memory Guild didn't deter me. He was an experienced actor. It was possible he didn't know the exact name of the guild. I didn't care. He had the motive and the army to attack us, so he was still our primary suspect in my eyes.

I drove to his mansion and parked across the street to spend a few boring hours watching. The only movement was his giant American flag fluttering from the large flagpole out front. I was getting sleepy.

Until movement caught my eye. Two thugs in sport coats emerged from the house and got into one of the giant black SUVs. I recognized the one who had challenged me when I trespassed. Compared to all the inaction I had sat through over the past days, this was big excitement. Even though Mewling wasn't with them, I decided to follow.

They went north on A1A until they turned onto the east-west road that went over the historic stone bridge into downtown San Marcos. I was glad they drove a colossal vehicle. Even when cars got between us, I never lost sight of their SUV.

We passed through the tourist zone and soon entered the neighborhood that was home to the small liberal arts college, where I had gotten my degree and where Dr. Noordlun was the Chair of the History Department.

Wasn't that risky—brazenly coming onto the territory of their prey?

They turned onto a side street and then into the entrance of a parking garage. They must have a parking pass, because the gate opened right up for them, and they drove through. The gate arm didn't rise for me; I had to pay. I considered backing out and waiting on the street. It would be risky following them in the close confines of the garage, but I needed to see what they were up to.

As I was fumbling in my purse for the bills to pay for my ticket, the SUV came down the ramp and went through the exit to my left. They hadn't even parked. And I thought I saw someone in the backseat, though it was tough to tell through the tinted windows. I apologized to the gate attendant and backed out.

I lost the SUV. I was too late in leaving the garage. Just in case, I headed back to the bridge, and while I waited at a red light, I saw the SUV crossing the bridge. They were most likely returning to Mewling's house, so that's where I went. By the time I arrived in my usual spot across the street, the SUV had already parked, and its occupants had gone inside. I missed seeing, for sure, if they had a passenger.

Hours went by until it was nearing Teatime at the inn. I wanted to wait here and see who the passenger was. My other housekeeper, Bella, was on duty, and I asked her to cover tea for me. I didn't feel as confident about her, but I had no choice.

Unfortunately, I waited until sundown, and no one left the house. Bella would be leaving for the day and I needed to get back to the inn to set out the wine and cheese.

The throaty roar arose of a classic MG convertible. Diego pulled up beside me. You think it's a cliche that a vampire would drive an antique car? Sorry, but a lot of them do. When you live forever, your tastes don't change with every ephemeral trend. Good, well-made machines are worth keeping around.

"Anything new?" Diego said through his window. He had pulled up with his hood beside my trunk so our driver's windows would be next to each other, the way cops do.

"I believe they have a visitor," I said. "They picked up someone in the parking garage at the college, but I couldn't see them in the backseat with the tinted windows."

Diego nodded. "When it gets later, I'll sneak up to the house and hopefully see or hear what's going on."

"Be careful. His bodyguards have guns."

"My dear, I have been on this property—on the roof, even— every night I've surveilled the place. No one has seen me, though I had to mesmerize a fellow once."

"What does Mewling do every night?"

"He's watching cable news or on the computer. That's it. I've never seen him pick up a book. And he goes to bed early, which is good for me, so I can return to my restaurant. Or go hunting for a bite to eat."

He gave me an evil smile. I cringed.

"Let me know right away if anything happens," I said before saying goodnight.

I didn't hear from Diego, so when it was approaching my bedtime, I called him. It went straight to voicemail. He had turned off his phone, probably so he could prowl around. I left a message telling him I was going to bed in a half hour.

Twenty minutes later, my phone rang.

"I have nothing major to report," Diego said, "but I was able to confirm Mewling has a guest. A woman friend, whom he dined with and shared a bed. I didn't get a good look at her, but she is not a young bimbo like one might have suspected. She has short brown hair and is in her forties or older. And, yes, his wife has been away all week."

When I awoke in the morning, I found a text from Diego saying that he had stayed until as close to dawn as he dared, but the guest hadn't left.

By the time I arrived at the mansion a couple of hours after dawn, my heart sank. One of the SUVs was gone. It returned to the house shortly after I arrived, with only the two bodyguards getting out.

I guessed they had given the woman a ride home and I, stupidly, had missed my chance to follow.

I spent a couple more hours sitting there in my car, but figured it would be a waste of time to stick around longer. I had chores to do, and I wanted to make finger sandwiches for tea, and canapés for the wine serving, since my offerings had been so minimal while I'd been playing detective.

I did find some time to get on the internet, though. I searched the sleazy tabloid sites for any word about Mewling's affair. But I came up with nothing. It gave me an extra appreciation for Jen's skills in gossip mongering.

"Jen," I said when I got her on the line, "do you know anything at all about this affair Mewling is having?"

"I told you all I know," she said.

"Would it help you think of suspects, if she was not a young bimbo but was older?"

"It opens the possibility that it's a married woman. But remember, I don't travel in Mewling's circle. All the gossip I get is second hand. I'll have to make more inquiries."

I thanked her and clicked off. I realized we needed a new plan. Getting evidence of an affair in order to blackmail Mewling into calling off his dogs was not going to work. Even if it did, it would not be enough. He needed to be held accountable for Gloria's attack and all the attempted ones. Blackmailing him about his affair wouldn't force him to confess to the police. Even if he lost his wife and half his money, he wouldn't put himself in prison.

We needed evidence. I reluctantly realized that Samson and Lepore were right, theorizing was a waste of time. Hard evidence was all that mattered.

The next day, I drove to Mewling's house once again, feeling hopeless, but not knowing what else to do. Maybe we could hack into his computer and look for incriminating emails? Yeah, I guess. Beats any other idea I had.

It was difficult to think with a siren approaching along A1A from behind me, I wished it would get past me already. But it didn't.

The red ambulance turned into Mewling's driveway. The security gates opened, and the vehicle pulled up to the house. Another siren screamed in my ear as a firetruck arrived and went up the driveway, parking near the ambulance. A police car showed up soon afterward.

About thirty minutes later, the paramedics pushed a gurney out of the house and into the ambulance. I couldn't see the patient's face even with my binoculars, but the enormous stomach jutting up beneath the sheet was unmistakable.

My fears were justified an hour later when I got the first news alert on my phone.

Lance Mewling was dead. The cause of death had not been released by the authorities, but the article hinted it was a heart attack or cardiac arrest.

My bad guy was gone.

SAM SPADE

Lance Mewling would not face justice. I had to accept that. I had to move on. His deluded followers were still out there, but hopefully, they'd find other conspiracy theories to occupy themselves.

And there would be no one telling them to kill members of The Memory Guild.

The police were still investigating the attempts on the Guild members. They finally located and arrested Gloria's strangler. Her first attacker, the guy strapped with too much gear, was also in jail, as was James' attacker, Diego's attempted bomber, and the driver for the man who shot at me. Dr. Noordlun's attempted killer became chum after going through the shrimp processing machine.

It was an impressive show of force to convince this many men to kill people for you, especially if, according to the driver's memories, you're not paying them. Maybe, that's where the supernatural came in.

In any event, they were all incompetent, except for the

person who strangled Gloria and almost finished the job. Monique sounded competent, and most likely would have killed me if she hadn't been off her game after she accidentally killed her husband. Sure, the others were enthusiastic, but that wasn't enough. Mewling got what he paid for.

I could try to locate the gunman who shot at me, but I had grown tired of playing amateur detective. I'll let Lepore hunt him down. I needed to focus on the inn and the constant repairs and renovations that come with the territory, when you buy an almost 300-year-old building.

I also needed to step up my marketing. I couldn't survive if thirty-six percent occupancy was a good day. I was learning how to do internet advertising, but it would be great if a prestigious travel magazine featured the inn. Yeah, right. Dream on.

Meanwhile, I prepared for a Mr. Sam Spade to arrive from Crescent City, Florida. He had booked the Princess Suite online and would arrive today.

I'd never had single male guests staying on their own before. Perhaps, he had a partner he didn't mention in the online form. Also, the Princess Suite, with its pink wallpaper and Chippendale-style furniture, was an odd choice for a guy, regardless of his sexual orientation. But who was I to question a paying customer, even if he was staying for only two nights?

Julie freshened up the linens in the suite, Room 204. She also dusted and vacuumed, which weren't needed, but I asked her to do it, anyway. I busied myself with the breakfast service, the one amenity that all guests took advantage of. After I cleaned up, the inn was ready. Clean and sparkling with the scent of old polished wood, a pleasant mustiness of old drapes, and the warmth of butter and baked goods.

A loud rumble came from Cadiz Street, the side street where the main entrance was located. There was a length along the curb of no parking, where guests could pull up to unload luggage before finding a parking spot elsewhere.

I looked out the window. An old pickup on monster tires idled by the entrance, belching exhaust. Mr. Spade?

The rumbling ceased and a large man extricated himself from the cab, using a metal step to make the long descent from the raised cab of the monster truck. He walked stiffly to the passenger side and pulled out a large suitcase. He wheeled the bag up the ramp to the inn.

The bell above the door tinkled.

"Good morning," I said, beaming with all the charm I could muster as I entered the foyer. "Are you Mr. Spade?"

"Yep, that's me."

Mr. Spade veered into cliche territory. He was tall with an enormous gut, cowboy boots, and jeans that lacked a waist to cling to beneath his stomach bulge. Clad in a black T-shirt and leather vest, he was bald, and had a beard atop his chubby cheeks so large it could be home to a family of mice. A toothpick protruded from this nest of gray hair.

This man will not be happy with the Princess Suite, I thought.

"Welcome to the Esperanza Inn," I said, beckoning him into the front room where the desk was. "How was your drive up here?"

"Good. I spotted a buck feeding in a clearing near the road, and his carcass is in the back of my truck. Do you have a refrigerator with room for several pounds of venison? I'll give you some."

"I'm sure we can accommodate you." I wasn't sure, but hoped my second fridge could handle it.

I asked for his credit card for incidental costs during his stay.

He pulled out two hundred-dollar bills.

"I made the reservation with my corporate card. This should cover any costs here, as long as I get the difference back."

This wasn't standard procedure, but since I wasn't part of a corporate chain, I could bend my own rules.

"Mr. Spade, are you sure you'll be happy in the Princess Suite?" I asked. "It's rather dainty."

"You got a problem with that?" he asked.

"Not at all. I just want you to be comfortable."

"I want to be wowed."

I handed him the wooden disc with the key to 204 attached.

"Afternoon tea is served at three. Wine and cheese will come out around five. Breakfast tomorrow runs from seven to ten. I hope you enjoy your stay. The elevator is just past the stairs."

I had doubts the elevator could support his weight. At least, I had good insurance.

He thanked me and rolled his suitcase toward the elevator, the wooden floor creaking as he went.

Once the relief of having another paying guest diminished slightly, I had some qualms as I stood up from the desk. I had to admit that Mr. Spade checked every box on the criteria for being a member of The Truth Squad.

Was I being prejudiced? Simply because he looked like he belonged to an armed militia didn't mean he did. He's just a country boy, here to do some antiquing in the quaint shops of San Marcos while sampling gourmet bites in the charming cafes. I had to stop being so paranoid. And remember, Lance Mewling was dead.

I banished such worries from my mind and went about my business. At 3:00 p.m., I wheeled the cart into the dining room, which I called the breakfast room.

The only guests in attendance were the two elderly sisters in

102, and Mr. Sam Spade. He smiled at me from the small table as his butt overflowed from the chair.

"Mr. Spade, how do you like your accommodations?" I asked as I poured hot water into his cup.

"It's gorgeous," he said. He grabbed a bag of Earl Grey from the tea box and pointed toward the blueberry scones and the egg salad finger sandwiches. I heaped them on his plate.

I attempted to read his thoughts, but I couldn't get through. Except, I did pick up a stray question about whether it would be piggish to request more finger sandwiches. And that was cool with me.

After I served the sisters, Mr. Spade called me back twice for more scones. Loving my scones moved him up a few notches in my opinion of him.

I was similarly surprised to see Mr. Spade at the wine serving. Often, guests grabbed glasses of wine and brought them up to their rooms instead of mingling with others like I had intended. But Mr. Spade stood there, sipping a Chardonnay, talking about animal husbandry with the German gentleman in 304.

I was feeling guilty for stereotyping Mr. Spade. I chalked this up as a life lesson.

This had been a good day. My guests were happy. There had been no complaints or problems. The supernatural residents of the inn had behaved themselves and stayed out of sight.

I went to sleep in my cottage with a smile on my face.

SAGE WAS NEXT TO MY BED TELLING ME TO WAKE UP. I assumed it was a dream.

Until my front door crashed open. I sat up in bed, panicking, as heavy footsteps moved through the front rooms.

I had to admit that I wasn't completely surprised. Were you?

My bedroom door burst open just as I bent to retrieve the baseball bat from under my bed.

Muzzle flashes came from a pistol fitted with a suppressor. Two holes sprouted in my pillow with feathers scattering.

I dove to the floor and rolled with the bat held close to my chest.

Sam Spade stepped into the room and tried to get me in his sights. His boots got tangled in my fluffy throw rug and he went down on the floor like a felled redwood, just missing me.

I jumped up and slammed the wooden bat on his head. It made a cartoonish "bonk" noise on his skull. I felt queasy at inflicting violence on someone. Just in case, I kicked the gun from his hand like they do in movies.

I stepped around his unconscious body and found my phone, calling 911 and reporting the attack.

Mr. Spade had looked like a Truth Squad member. Thank heavens, he was also incompetent like one.

I was still on the call when the giant body on my floor moved. I shrieked and accidentally dropped the phone.

A large hand reached for my ankle. I bashed it with the bat.

But Mr. Spade slowly gathered his bulk and rose to his feet. He found the gun on the floor.

And I ran.

No one thinks logically when chased by a four-hundred-pound man with a gun. I should have run out of the courtyard and into the street where, even at this hour, people would hear my screams.

But I didn't think of this until I was already inside the inn, with the killer lumbering inside after me.

I couldn't go out the main door because he would cut me off. I thought about exiting through the unused door in the front room, but it had a habit of sticking. It was a fire hazard, I admit. And a murder hazard.

A shot went off behind me. It wasn't very silent, despite the silencer. I ran upstairs without thinking, cursing myself for leading the killer into my inn where innocent guests were sleeping.

I raced up the stairs toward the third floor, hoping Mr. Spade would get a heart attack. Or at least be too exhausted to reach me before the police showed up.

Somehow, he was gaining on me. My scones must have given him extra stamina.

I crossed the landing on the second floor and started up the stairs to the third. The thud of his footsteps reached the second-floor landing.

The elevator doors squeaked open on the second floor. What the heck? Everyone knows you don't take the elevator during a fire or a murderous redneck rampage.

I should cut the power and trap him in there.

Problem was, the circuit breakers were down in the kitchen.

I reached the third floor just before he did. The elevator door opened around the corner behind the staircase.

I could lock myself in a bedroom and cower while he smashed the door open. Or I could run back downstairs.

A third option presented itself. The door to the attic was right in front of me.

A door that didn't really exist, to the attic that didn't exist. Sometimes, it appeared as a trapdoor in the third-floor ceiling, the kind you had to pull open with a pole and extend a folding ladder. Other times, it looked like this: a closet door in the hallway.

A bullet hole appeared in the drywall next to my head. The hallway floor shook as the killer lumbered toward me.

I didn't think. I just opened the door and ascended the dark staircase of unfinished wood, instantly becoming nauseous from approaching the gateway between worlds.

The gateway to the In Between.

My cousin, Missy, told me she had been there with a dragon she had rescued who was searching for his mother. Dragons regularly took shelter in the In Between, because they couldn't safely live on earth any longer.

Humans didn't go to the In Between. Only the souls of the dead, in limbo between earth and Heaven, went there.

It was too dangerous for living humans, Missy told me. She advised me to never go through this door.

But I also wondered if Cory, my missing second husband, had gone to the In Between. There were clues indicating he had. I wondered if he was trapped there and needed to be rescued.

I was halfway up the dark stairs when the door to the hallway below opened and light flooded in.

Right, I couldn't forget I had a psycho with a gun coming after me.

I ran up the stairs until they took a ninety-degree turn to the left. My nausea increased and a tingling sensation filled my body.

A dim light glowed at the top of this flight of stairs, and the air shimmered in front of it as if I were looking through a water-fall. I climbed closer.

A stair creaked behind me.

And I stepped into the gateway to the In Between.

CHAPTER 16

THE IN BETWEEN

It was like falling a good six feet. I hit the ground with a jolt, sending my knees into my stomach and knocking the wind out of me. After wheezing in big gulps of air, I looked around.

I was in a grassy, high-plains territory. Waves of undulating hills, all covered in grass, stretched as far as I could see. In the far distance was a wall of snow-capped mountains. I didn't know what compass direction it was.

Because there was no visible sun. The amount of light on the hills resembled that of a sunny day. But in the sky, there was no orb of light. Instead, the sky was like a white dome, uncomfortable to the eyes.

The temperature was pleasant. There was no wind. I felt as if I were in the artificial environment of a terrarium.

I got to my feet and turned 360 degrees. Thankfully, Mr. Sam Spade was not running toward me. Neither was any other human nor animal nor insect. I reached down and plucked a blade of grass, squashed it between my fingers and smelled it. It seemed real.

So, what was I supposed to do here? Wander randomly for miles and look for Cory? How would I get home? How would I find food and water?

Missy had never explained those details to me, but it sounded like she had never been here long enough to worry about sustenance.

The highest ground was to my right, although it didn't seem much higher than where I was now. I walked there, hoping to get a better view of my surroundings. I climbed up and down smaller hills before I ascended the slope of the largest one.

I did get a better view up here. But it was of more of the same landscape. More grassy hills stretching to the horizons or to the mountains. The grass varied in darkness, as if some hills got more rain than others. But that was the only thing breaking up the monotony of the landscape.

I didn't know where to go, but I had to go somewhere. So I decided to head for the mountains, even though they could be days of walking away. Maybe, there was no such thing as day and night here.

Interestingly, I still had my watch and my phone with me. I took my phone from my pocket. It was dead and wouldn't start up. My watch was my grandmother's old analog wristwatch, the kind you had to wind up. It wasn't working, either. I wound it up, and it started ticking again, but I didn't know what the actual time was.

I began my march. With my watch working again, I can tell you I walked for over two hours and nothing changed about the landscape. And the mountains didn't seem any closer. The only difference was I was more tired and, now, thirsty. I had no choice but to keep going.

"Hey! Wait up!" The voice came from far behind me.

It was a familiar voice, and my blood froze.

Sure enough, Sam Spade was scrambling over the hills trying to catch up to me.

I took off at a jog away from him.

"It's okay, I won't hurt you. We have to stick together here. Wait up!"

Yeah, right. There was no way I would trust him.

I kept going, glancing back from time to time. He seemed to be gaining on me ever so slightly. After all, he had a much longer stride, but he should tire out before I did. Though, he hadn't so far. I wondered if he still had his gun and if it would work in this world.

It occurred to me I could never rest or sleep in this world knowing that man was here, too.

"You're not being very nice," he shouted. "Wait for me, please."

I kept going, and the landscape remained the same. Except now, there were shadows on the grass of birds circling overhead. The only animals in this world were vultures.

But, no, they weren't vultures. Silhouetted against the bright white sky were six brown-green dragons. Each had four legs tucked up against its stomach, a serpentine tail with a forked end streaming behind it, and two giant leathery wings beating the air.

I should have been shocked to see dragons. But I was well beyond capable of feeling shock.

The dragons were studying me and Spade, too. I hoped they weren't hungry.

One of them swooped down to only about thirty feet above the ground. The wind from its wings buffeted me, and I screamed.

I looked up to catch the dragon's eye as it hovered above me.

It was a highly intelligent gaze. It appraised me in a knowing manner.

The wind struck me as the dragon flapped hard and banked in a turn. Now, it was hovering over Spade. The man changed course and tried to run away from the beast.

I'll find out if he has his gun, I thought.

There were no gunshots. I continued moving, at more of a fast walk than a jog.

A hideous scream came from behind me.

The dragon climbed into the sky with Spade dangling from its talons like a rodent captured by a hawk.

Spade flailed and twisted to free himself from the dragon's grip, but it was at high enough altitude that Spade would be killed if he fell. I tried, but I couldn't feel sorry for the man.

The dragon flew with his prize to his brethren who still circled above. They sniffed the human, seemed to come to some agreement, and the six dragons circled downward until they disappeared behind a nearby rise.

More agonizing screams came. Then, all was silent. I kept on walking, trying not to think about what just happened.

Several minutes later, the same dragon, who had studied me before, appeared overhead. I recognized him from the flaws in his scale armor, the broken tip of a head horn, and the wise expression in his eyes.

He turned to face me with both eyes, hovering just above me.

"No, please don't!" I shouted.

A man's voice entered my head, speaking in English.

Don't be afraid. We will not harm you. It was a true telepathic connection, but one that I didn't have to seek out.

You are one of the gifted humans, the dragon said in my mind. *We consider you a friend. The other one,* he pointed his head toward where they had disappeared with Spade, *was a predator and meant you harm. Those like him are not welcome here in our refuge.*

The dragon flew several yards ahead of me. I stopped walking as he lowered himself to the ground with flapping that sent dirt and grass scattering. He folded his wings atop his back, arched his sinuous neck, and took a few steps toward me.

He towered over me like a dinosaur. But I tried to not be afraid.

What do you seek here in the In Between? the dragon asked telepathically.

I was trying to escape from that predator, I answered telepathically. You know, when in Rome. *But I'm also curious if my husband is here. He walked through a door that disappeared, and I never saw him again.*

Humans don't live here, only souls.

But I'm here.

You cannot survive here without magic. The only humans who can spend extended time here are magicians: witches, wizards, mages, and the like. They must use their magic to sustain themselves, and only temporarily.

How do you dragons live here?

We have magic. And we also pop back to earth to eat some cows or humans now and then.

I wondered if Cory had a magical ability that he or I wasn't aware of. Or perhaps a magician here would be feeding him?

Where can I find any humans who are here? I asked.

There are very few who stay here for long periods. You should go. You have some magic in you, but not enough to create food and water. I can find a gateway for you, so you can return.

Thank you, but I wish to speak to one of these magicians.

So be it. I will take you.

Um, I'd rather not be carried dangling from your talons. Can I ride on your back like in the fantasy books?

The dragon seemed to laugh. That is, if dragons are capable of that.

No one rides on my back. And this is the In Between. There are better ways to traverse this world, because it is always transforming. Face this way.

He gestured with his snout toward the mountains. I did what he said.

Turn one step to your right, he said. One step more. Now walk in a straight line until you get to where you're going.

I didn't understand. But I did what he said. Ever since I'd been here, I felt as if I were dreaming. So, in the logic of dreams, anything could happen. I'd much prefer to wake up and find myself in my bed, but considering what just happened in my bedroom, I was willing to go with this particular dream logic.

I focused on the grass ahead of me, imagining a straight line, and walked up a gradual incline to the top with more identical hills ahead of me. I felt somewhat nauseous. Before I went downhill, I glanced behind me.

The dragons were no longer there.

Oddly, I missed them. I was all alone in this strange world again, one in which I would die of thirst and starvation if I stayed too long.

I turned to face forward again and continue my path. And I was stunned.

Before me lay an entirely different landscape. The hill I was on descended to a large lake. To the left of the lake was a forest that seemed to stretch to the mountains, which were still there. The rolling hills extended to my side of the lake. And on the far distant shore of the lake to my right was more forest.

I felt obligated to continue walking in a straight line. As I neared the lakeshore, small trees and bullrushes came into view. To my left, between the forest's edge and the lake, I thought I saw structures. My heart quickened. Yes, there were huts made of branches. I saw wisps of smoke. I began jogging toward this encampment, my heart yearning for someone to help me.

When I reached the camp, though, I was disappointed. There was no campfire and food cooking. The smoke I had seen came from a flat rock on the ground with nothing visible on it to create a fire. There were only tendrils of smoke curling up from the rock's surface. Four thatched huts made of branches and grass sat here and there haphazardly.

"Is anyone here?" I called in a quaking voice. My mouth was dry. I needed some water.

A man crawled out of a hut. He wore a crude leather jacket and trousers plus a beaver fur cap.

"Are you an ordinary human?" he asked in a heavy French accent, crouching at the entrance to his hut.

"I don't like to think of myself as ordinary."

"No, do you have magic?"

"I am a telepath and a psychometrist. But I am not a magician."

"Then, what are you doing here?"

"I came here by mistake. I stumbled through a gateway, if that's what you call it."

"Then, *mais oui*, you must stumble back."

"I need to know if you've seen my husband. He also stumbled through a gateway, and I haven't seen him since."

"Is he a magician?"

"Not that I'm aware of. But he might have abilities he's not aware of either."

"What is his name?"

"Cory Slaughter. He's tall with longish, straight brown hair parted on the side.

"I have not seen him." He turned toward the huts. "*Mes amis*! Come out and help this semi-ordinary woman."

Straw rustled, and three other people crawled from their crude huts. One was an elderly Native American, thin and wearing trousers, suspenders, and a red shirt that did not look contemporary. The next to emerge was a young woman in a long, black woolen dress and a gray cap covering her hair and tied beneath her chin. The last to emerge was a heavy woman around my age with leather pants (shiny, not raw leather like the Frenchman's), a black T-shirt and a purple mohawk.

The four of them stared at me like I was Bigfoot or something.

"Hi," I said. "I'm Darla Chesswick from Planet Earth. Specifically, San Marcos, Florida. Have you guys seen a man named Cory Slaughter? Tall guy, straight brown hair parted on the side?"

No one answered.

"We are refugees," the middle-aged punk rocker said. "We tend to avoid people."

"Refugees from what?"

"Oppression and cruelty," said the young woman. "In my village, they were burning witches. Innocent, pure girls, they were. But I was a true witch, in fact. I fled my village and found a gateway that brought me here to safety."

"When did you flee?" I asked, looking at her old-fashioned clothing. "I mean, what year?"

"The year of our Lord sixteen sixty-five."

I was dumbstruck. "Are you immortal? That was hundreds of years ago."

"No, it is still the sixteen-sixties. I return to True Earth from time to time, so I can assure you this is so."

"There is no such thing as time here in the In Between," the

Native American said. "We each still exist in the era from which we fled."

"You all escaped persecution because of your magic?" I asked.

They nodded.

"How do you survive here?"

"We create food and water with our magic," the Frenchman said. "Nothing is completely real here. The water in the lake is not real. Even our shelter," he pointed to the huts. "These materials are not real, but they feel like they are to us and give us comfort."

I was having a hard time comprehending.

"I don't understand what this world is."

"It's not a world," the Native American said. "It's a land among the stars where the gods and monsters live along with the souls of our ancestors."

"It's like another dimension, or plane of existence," the punk rocker said. "Little Bear was right, though, about what lives here. Souls of the dead who have not made it to Heaven or Hell. There are monsters like dragons and kraken who take refuge here from the modern world, just as we do. And there are ancient gods who are no longer remembered in modern times. It's best to avoid running into them."

"Do you live here permanently?" I asked.

The four exchanged glances like I'd touched upon a sore subject.

"We must always return from where we came," said the Frenchman. "For short visits, at least."

"We have to do that to maintain our existence. Our human forms, I guess," the punk rocker said. "If we stayed here, we'd die and fade into nothingness. We can create food with our magic, but we can't maintain our physical existence forever like this."

The four didn't seem happy about this truth.

"It is dangerous to return," said the Frenchman. "But we must. We have no choice."

"What about me?" I asked. "How long can I stay? And does anyone have some water to spare?"

The Native American man chanted words in his indigenous tongue and a gourd filled with water appeared in his open hand. He handed it to me.

It was fresh and cool. Was it truly water? It surely seemed like it as I chugged it down.

"Thank you," I said. "So have none of you seen my husband?"

"I have," the young Puritan woman said.

They all looked at her in surprise, no one more surprised than I.

"Really?" I asked. "When and where?"

"There is no when and where here," she said in a soft voice. "Remember, we are refugees. We are always on the move. The four of us here have never seen each other before this visit. But once before, in the In Between, I saw a man like you describe. Does he have blue eyes?"

"Yes," I said, my heart swelling. "And a dimpled chin?"

She nodded. "He arrived in the camp I was staying in at the time. Just as you have. But a wizard among us discovered your husband has magic in his blood. The wizard agreed to train him."

"Did my husband want to return to me?"

She nodded. "He did. But there were reasons he could not. I do not know what they were, except, perhaps, that he wanted to stay for training. I left the camp shortly after he arrived, so I know not what befell of him."

All this had totally—what's the clinical term?—blown my mind. Passing through a portal to another world was freaky enough. But now, I was hearing confirmation that my husband didn't bail on me deliberately. He stumbled into the In Between, just like I had. And he survived. At least, for a while. Toss into this crazy mix the fact he had magic in his blood, and I was about to lose my little remaining sanity.

"Thank you," I said to the young woman, "for confirming that Cory was here. And thank all of you for your water and help."

"You think you're just going to walk home?" the punk rocker asked.

"I haven't figured that out yet."

"You need help to find a gateway," the Frenchman said. "And you must not travel alone here in the In Between."

"Because of the dragons? They're cool with me."

"There are many other dangerous creatures here," said the Native American man. "I will take you to a gateway. We will leave now. The one that brought you here may still be nearby."

"I'll go with you," the punk rocker said. "I have a good sense for finding gateways."

I drank the remaining water in the gourd and nodded.

"I'm ready."

The elderly Native American man walked with the aid of a staff. The punk rocker carried one, too, a gnarled, sturdy-looking stick, though she didn't use it for walking. We traveled along the lakeshore.

"Are there edible fish in there?" I asked.

The punk rocker laughed. "There are creatures in there, but they are not edible. They would be happy to eat you, though."

"You make all your food with magic?"

"Everything you see here is an illusion. It's either temporary or not what it appears to be."

"I don't understand."

"The branches we used to make our shelters aren't from real

trees. They'll fade away in time. This staff will last only because I preserved it with magic."

"You said if you stay here too long, you will die and fade away. Can you explain?"

"If you haven't figured it out yet, this world isn't real. It's just a temporary transfer point between worlds. The food and water we create isn't real. The air we breathe isn't real either. I don't know why it's here for us to breathe. But eventually, reality catches up to the living, mortal creatures that come here. Your body will fail. Your cells will come apart."

"Have you ever seen this happen to someone?"

"I did once. Sort of like a melting snowman. It wasn't pretty. You need to return to the world you came from to prevent that, to reconstitute your cell structure, I guess. After that, you can return here. If you still want to."

"Why did you come here, if you don't mind my asking?"

The woman held up her hand and stopped. She stared out at the lake for a moment, then turned and gazed at the grassy hills.

"I feel a gateway not far away," she said. "I think it's this way."

She strode up a gentle slope.

"You're seeking a man," she said to me without looking at me. "I came here to escape one. Either he would have killed me, or I would have killed him. At the time, this seemed like a better idea."

"Did you have magic on earth?" I asked.

"Yes. But I didn't know how to use it. My friends here taught me. When I'm ready, I'll return home and use it to correct the situation I ran away from."

I didn't want to know any details.

"I'm Darla, by the way."

"I'm Fran. And this is Little Bear."

"If I ever come back here, how can I find you?"

Fran finally looked at me then. "I don't recommend you come back here."

We walked forever, though I had no way to tell for sure how long. The landscape continued to be the monotonous undulating grassy hills. I wondered how Fran thought she could find the gateway out here.

Little Bear gave a low whistle and stopped. He and Fran crouched and looked around warily. I did the same, unsure of what I was looking out for.

Suddenly, Little Bear leaped forward and swung his staff above his head. It made a *crunch* as it hit something invisible. He jumped backward, surprisingly agile for an old man.

Then a cockroach appeared. A giant cockroach. I mean, a cockroach the size of a minivan. And it was angry.

Both Little Bear and Fran hit it with their staffs. An arc of electricity flowed from each staff, meeting in the middle and then spreading over the roach.

A burning smell hit my nose and the cockroach disappeared, along with the odor.

"Was that real?" I asked.

"Real enough to harm you," Fran said. "That's just one of the many reasons I don't advise coming to the In Between."

"And now I know where cockroaches disappear to when you turn the light on," I said.

They didn't laugh at my joke. Probably, because what I said was true.

"A gateway is near," Fran said, "I can sense it."

I had an uneasy feeling, which I thought was from the giant cockroach, but as we climbed the next hill, nausea swept over me. A gateway truly was nearby.

On the other side of the summit, the air shimmered in an

area with a ten-foot diameter. The closer we got, the opaquer the circle became and the more ill I felt.

"Fran and I must not get closer," Little Bear said. "Have a safe journey."

"Thank you."

I shook his and Fran's hands. Their hands were colder to the touch than they should have been, at least on earth.

"If you see my husband, please tell him to come home."

"We will," Fran said.

I stepped into the gateway and shuddered from a blast of icy air as my body left this dimension, and my innards felt like they went through a blender. Darkness engulfed me.

Pain shot through my hands and knees as I landed hard on wood. Two-by-fours. I touched attic insulation.

Then, I fell further as a crack of light yawned into daylight, and I swung downwards, my staircase coming into view. I realized I was atop the folding ladder of a trapdoor to the attic that didn't exist. The trapdoor dropped open. The ladder didn't unfold. And I tumbled down into the hallway, landing hard on the carpeted floor.

Nothing felt broken. I looked up and the trapdoor wasn't there. The ceiling was smooth and white, with no visible seams showing an opening.

So much for a dignified homecoming.

CHAPTER 17

EVERYONE LOVES SHIPLAP

Footsteps thudded up the stairs below me.

"My Lord! Darla! What are you doing here?" It was Julie. "We thought you'd been kidnapped! How did you escape?"

"I had a little help."

"And what are you doing falling on the floor of the third-floor hallway?"

"I like over-the-top entrances?"

She bent over me and fussed like a hen. "Let me help you up. Are you okay?"

"Thank you," I said as I stood up. I could have done it on my own, but she was yanking on my arms. I needed to regain some dignity here.

"The police just left," Julie said. "They called me after they arrived, and I came straight over. After you called nine-one-one, the guests heard gunshots and called nine-one-one, too. The police talked to all the guests, but the new one in two-oh-four is missing. They figured he attacked you and kidnapped you.

They're out looking for him. But now, here you are, only an hour or so after the police arrived."

"Only an hour?" I asked. I had been in the In Between for several hours, at least.

Julie nodded. "Were you hiding in a closet up here?"

"No, I must have gotten home without you seeing me," I lied. "I came up here to inspect the bullet holes, and I guess I passed out. Too much adrenaline, I guess."

"Who attacked you?"

"Sam Spade, the guest in two-oh-four. He broke into my cottage, shot at me, and chased me up here before he caught me and dragged me out to his pickup."

"How did you escape?"

"I jumped out of the truck at a red light."

She looked at me dubiously. "You should call the police and tell them you're free, and that they need to look for that man."

I wanted to say that no one was ever going to find that man, but I couldn't.

"Thanks, Julie. What time is it? My watch and phone died."

"Three-forty a.m."

I still couldn't get over the discrepancy, that I had been in the In Between for so many hours, but only one had passed here.

Since my cellphone wouldn't start up again, I called Detective Lepore from the inn's landline. She didn't answer, which wasn't surprising at this hour. I tried Samson next.

"Darla, are you okay?"

"Yes, now that you finally called me by my first name."

"I'm serious. I was scared to death for you. What the heck happened?"

Samson was more accepting of the supernatural than other cops. Being a werewolf did that to you. But I couldn't tell him *everything.* I lost him the moment I tried to explain about the other plane of existence.

"Where's the guy who attacked you, this Sam Spade character? That's obviously not his real name, by the way. Haven't you read Dashiell Hammett or seen *The Maltese Falcon?*"

I felt stupid that I hadn't realized that myself. I needed to brush up on my classic detective stories.

"He never came back from the In Between," I said. "He had, shall we say, a fatal accident over there."

"Did you do it?"

"Honestly, I did not. He was killed by very large reptiles."

"Gators?"

"Yes. Gators."

"I was hoping we'd catch him and be able to interrogate him. I'm assuming he was another of the assassins."

"Yes, but if Lance Mewling is dead, why was someone still trying to kill me? He must have received the orders before Mewling's heart attack."

"Or maybe your theory about Mewling is just flat out wrong."

"That's not what I want to hear right now."

"It's not my job to tell you what you want to hear. Remember, I warned you about theorizing without having evidence."

"I don't know who else would want to kill my friends and me. Do you?"

I couldn't read minds over the phone. Not even over a land line. So I had to accept whatever he said.

"No, we don't have any other suspects at the moment. But I'll be looking out for you. Stay safe."

What he said at the end there made me feel good. I was surprised by how much it did. Still, I now was fairly certain my husband hadn't walked out on me deliberately. It made me want to leave the lamp on for him. But if he hadn't returned by now, why should I rekindle hope that he would in the future?

The time discrepancy with the In Between made me wonder. How long had he stayed there to learn magic? It had been a year since he disappeared. That would translate to several years in the In Between. He couldn't stay there that long and survive. He would need to have returned to earth to keep his body functioning. So, why he didn't find me while he was back here? He then went back to the In Between without having seen me?

Or did he simply return to earth and start a new life, not wanting to return to me? That was just as bad as walking out intentionally in the first place.

I was back to wanting to forget about him.

There were many other things to focus on, at least. I went to the front room downstairs. Archibald was frozen in stony sleep.

"Hey, Archibald, I have a question for you."

I didn't expect an immediate answer, and I didn't get one.

"Stone-head, could you please wake up?"

Nope. It was time to get nasty.

"Hey Archie-boy! You there, little Archie?"

The way he transformed from stone to a living creature always amazed me. At first, he looked like your average everyday gargoyle perched on a cathedral somewhere. Then, it was as if a photograph were projected upon the stone, looking as if there were two layers of his surface. Then the details of his demonic visage shifted ever so slightly, before becoming fully animated. He was a living, flesh-and-blood, angry gargoyle again.

"I thought I told you about calling me that name," he said.

"You did, but it seems that annoying you is the only way to get you to respond to me. Among humans, younger siblings use that technique."

He sighed, a rattling wind of ancient exasperation. "What do you want?"

"I have a couple of questions. Are you familiar with the In Between?"

He was surprised. "I am. I didn't think humans knew about it."

"My cousin, Missy, the witch, told me about it. I wasn't sure I believed in it. Until now. I just returned from there."

"Egads, that's unbelievable. I'm happy you could return. How did you get there?"

"There was a gateway on the third floor disguised as an attic. I've seen it appear before. Are you aware of that?"

"Not at all. I did sense instability in the energies while I was sleeping. It briefly woke me. But as far as I know, there have never been gateways in this house. Not before you moved here."

"Does that mean gateways follow me around? I think I had one in my home in Key West."

"I know about the In Between," Archibald said, "but I have never been there. In fact, I never intend to. But everyone knows gateways come and go. They're not attached to a single place. They can pop up anywhere."

"Can they be attached to a person?"

"I've never heard of that. It is odd, though, that you had one in two different homes."

"Yes. Odd."

"I'm afraid I can't help you any further. Except to warn you not to go through a gateway. It seems, however, you've already crossed that threshold."

"Good metaphor. Now, I have another question for you. Why isn't the Guild doing more to stop whoever is attacking us? I almost got killed again tonight."

"I heard the gunshots."

"And you did nothing to help me?"

"I would have if I could move more quickly. As to your first question, Dr. Noordlun and the rest agreed with your theory that Lance Mewling was behind the violence. We expected it would end with his death."

"Can we meet and discuss this, so we're not just waiting around like sitting ducks?"

"I will request a meeting."

If you want the truth about events that happened in the past, you turn to The Memory Guild. If you want to prevent events, you need to find someone else to help you.

I NEEDED TO GET SOME SLEEP. BUT BACK IN MY COTTAGE, seeing the bullet hole in my pillow and headboard was the opposite of a relaxation trigger. I paced around my small living quarters, trying to develop new theories without any evidence. Finally, I decided to violate a crime scene.

Technically, Spade's room was not a crime scene, since nothing illegal had happened there. Nevertheless, the police had covered the lock with a sticker so no potential evidence would be disturbed. I peeled off the sticker and used the passkey to walk right in.

This truly was a girly room with its decor. Who knows, maybe that was what drove Spade to violence. My bad joke aside, I was going to try to find out who ordered him to do it.

I glanced around the room, and my hopes faded. The room was empty. He must have packed up everything and put it in his pickup before he attacked me.

I already knew the outside doorknob had been corrupted

when I first turned it. Too many police hands had touched it since Spade had. I tried the inside knob. Same problem.

Doorknobs are usually touched only briefly, and people's thoughts while doing so are fleeting. The energy left upon the hardware is paltry, easily messed up by other people's hands.

The rare exception is when someone holds a doorknob for a longer time while having powerful emotions. That's why the memories of the murderous husband remain strong on the doorknob of 303. Powerful memories can exist on objects for hundreds of years, no matter how much they're handled afterwards. This is why psychometry is so fascinating.

I looked around the room, and the bed was untouched. The man obviously spent time here waiting to attack me. Aside from posting photos of his room to social media, what would he be doing? Reading a novel? Fat chance. So I picked up the television remote control. It was full of—

—still more time to kill. Got to make sure she's asleep before I go in. Thank God they're running a marathon of my favorite show . . . but I hate that wallpaper! No way! That's so barbarically loud! They should have picked a nice dark-floral pattern. Better yet, leave the wall unfinished and expose the shiplap. Everyone loves shiplap. Now, I really want to see how they stage this room. Such a tiny room with this loud wallpaper, they'll need to choose some dainty pieces, so the space isn't overpowered. Okay, on to the master bath . . . a bidet? That's marvelous! I think all Americans should adopt the bidet tradition. We need to be more like the French . . . but no! Not subway tile in the shower! No, please, no! That's so overdone these days. I thought she had better taste than that! I simply can't—

—stand being in this guy's inane head any longer. Is killing so easy for him that he doesn't even think about it beforehand? I was hoping to pick up his memories of getting the assignment, not his mindless commentary about HGTV.

I sighed with frustration. I was given the gifts of telepathy and psychometry, and there I was, no better off than the police.

I could read thoughts and memories. It's not my fault if they're stupid.

So where was the killer's truck? His steering wheel would hold much more helpful memories. Then again, they could be as trivial as the ones I just read. He didn't tell me where he parked and hadn't asked for reimbursement for a city parking lot fee, so I wouldn't know where it was unless the police found it. I would have to remember to give the police his license plate number from his room reservation. Assuming he didn't give a fake one.

This train of thought reminded me of my plan to find the Simpsons' car and try to read their memories.

WHEN I WOKE UP, CERVANTES WAS STANDING ON MY HIP, demanding to be fed. I wondered where he'd hid when I was attacked. He didn't seem the least bit traumatized today.

Cervantes was petite and sleek and pure-black, acting as if he owned the place ever since he first showed up a few months ago. He claimed my cottage and the courtyard as his territory, but occasionally, he snuck into the inn. When he did, I had to carry him out, in case any guests were allergic to cats.

Shortly after he had adopted me, I took him to the vet for shots and a flea bath. I was relieved to find out he didn't already have a microchip implanted by an owner who was missing him. I'd scoured the online missing-pet listings, and couldn't match him to a lost black cat with a notch in one ear. The notch meant he was a stray who'd been captured, fixed, and then released again.

So, Cervantes was missing both his manhood and a

microchip. The vet gave him a chip, and Cervantes was officially mine.

The vet estimated Cervantes to be around two years old. But he seemed wise beyond his years. In fact, it felt as if we already knew each other. And I mean that seriously.

"Cory, are you in that cat's body?" I asked Cervantes one day when he stared at me with striking familiarity.

"No," he meowed. His vocalizations often sounded like a drawn-out "no."

I didn't take the cat for his word. I'd make the judgement myself if my missing husband had somehow been turned into a cat.

And to clarify, Cory was *not* a shifter. The only shifter I knew was Samson, who tried to keep it a secret that he was a werewolf. Until I found out, that is.

Regardless of whether Cervantes had a human trapped inside him, he had an affinity for ghosts. When he snuck into the inn, he invariably headed straight for one of the haunted rooms, 202 or 303, and scratched at the doors to get in. Even when the rooms were unoccupied. Because the ghosts were permanent guests.

You already know about the ghost in 303. I recently discovered 202 had a ghost, too. An overweight Elvis impersonator who, when the inn was under different management, stayed here for a wedding and died of a heart attack in the room's hot tub.

Room 202 used to be called The Honeymoon Suite. Now, I call it The Fat-Elvis Suite. Or the Heartbreak Hotel Suite. But not in my brochures, of course.

I've heard a very convincing Elvis voice belting out his hits from the room at odd hours. Very few guests have complained. Most thought it was cool to stay in a haunted room with an unthreatening ghost, though some said I was faking it with a hidden sound system.

Cervantes believed in the ghosts, though. When I caught him scratching at the door, instead of carrying him outside right away, I would let him in (if the room was vacant). I'd watch him strut around with his tail sticking up, rubbing his cheeks on the furniture as he headed for the hot tub.

Then, he'd jump up onto the edge of the tub and let out a mournful yowl.

I couldn't tell if he was lamenting the death of the Elvis impersonator, or if he was channeling him and trying to sing "It's Now or Never." But it made the hairs on the back of my neck stand up.

Now, if I could only teach my new buddy how to sniff out assassins.

"HI, MOM."

Sophie appeared in the kitchen while I was preparing breakfast for the guests.

"Hello, dear," I said, turning away from the cutting board to give her a kiss on the cheek.

"I hate to ask again, but can I have fifty dollars?"

I turned back to the board and attacked the onions with my knife like I was chopping wood.

"I'll pay you back with my labor," she said. "You're short of help here, so I'll do anything you need—cleaning, cooking, serving breakfast. For as many hours as you think is fair."

I turned back to face her. Her color drained when she saw my expression.

"You're working full time at the restaurant. I know it's not great money, but you're living with Grammers, and she's not charging rent. Where is all your money going?"

"I still have a student loan I'm paying off."

"It all doesn't add up, Sophie. Look, I hate to ask this, but—"

"I'm not buying drugs, okay? You'll just have to trust me on this."

"Are you gambling?"

Sophie laughed. "You know that's not me."

"Are you giving all your money to political action committees? To an exiled Nigerian prince? Don't tell me you're giving it to your father?"

"No, to all the above. It's for a good cause, to help a friend. I promised I'd keep it secret, for now at least."

"Before you spend too much money on your friend, are you sure they're getting any assistance they're entitled to, like food stamps, or disability?"

She knew I was probing. And she wasn't falling for it.

"She's already doing all she can."

"What about one of those online fundraising campaigns?" I asked.

She smiled and shook her head. "Someday, I hope to explain."

I sighed theatrically. "I think I have fifty dollars on me."

I'm ashamed to say there wasn't any money in petty cash. Instead, I pulled the bills from my jeans pocket.

"Thanks, Mom. Just let me know when you want me to do the work," she said as she hugged me.

Then she took off.

CHAPTER 18

EUPHORIA

Detective Cynthia Lepore clicked off the phone call. The forensic examiner from the FBI's Jacksonville office had given her a suggestion that made her full of optimism.

The antique dagger, that was the murder weapon at the Esperanza Inn, had yielded no useful fingerprints, not even any partials. She sent a photo of the dagger to Jacksonville, asking if there were any other tests she could run. The forensic examiner noted that the dagger's handle, wrapped in small-diameter metallic wire, might have trapped exfoliated skin cells buried between the strands of wire that would not be easily detected.

Considering that the crime lab in San Marcos was what you'd expect in a small city, she agreed that evidence could have been missed. The FBI lab was willing to search for any overlooked biological material and run tests on the cells.

Lepore knew it might lead nowhere. But it could also bust open the dead-end case. She was exhilarated.

She took the stairs to the evidence room two floors below. At the front desk, the clerk handed her the request form, and then went back into the storage room to find the dagger. He came back a few minutes later with two sealed manilla envelopes. He gave her the heavier one, then a lighter one.

"The second one is a case that presumably held the weapon," he said. "Do you want both of them?"

She nodded. "Sure, why not?"

He gave her a second form to sign, and ten minutes later, she was driving out of the city toward the interstate for the hour-long trip to Jacksonville, the evidence sitting on the front passenger seat.

The evening rush hour had faded, and she merged onto I-95 smoothly. She relaxed as a tune ran through her head, so she had no desire to turn on the radio. She didn't remember what the song was, but it was so familiar and heartwarming. Was it a hymn from her youth? Possibly.

The song stuck with her as the miles flew by. It made her feel strong and righteous. Powerful, even.

She felt good having the dagger beside her, too. For some reason, it made her feel safer than her Glock did. She dwelt upon the memory of taking the package from the clerk and feeling how heavy it was: the weight of quality steel, as well as the precious metals and gems. The dagger would feel really good in her hand. It would be a joy to use that weapon, perfectly balanced in her hand, easy to maneuver, sharp as a razor, and as lethal as they come. She'd admired the crafts-manship of the weapon when she first saw it at the crime scene. It must have cost a fortune for whoever had first bought it.

A small blue sign announced a rest stop a mile ahead. She giggled. It was silly, but she wanted to examine the dagger more closely before she handed it off to the FBI lab. Just see how it felt in her hand. She'd wear latex gloves, of course. Sure, maybe this was bending the rules a bit, but there would be no harm. It would just take a minute.

She exited the highway and coasted into the rest stop, pulling into a space far from the restrooms and concessions. Turning on the interior dome light, she pulled two gloves from the dispenser box under her seat and put them on. She carefully opened the envelope without tearing it.

Man, the dagger felt glorious in her hand as she pulled it free. She switched off the light and brandished the weapon in her right hand. The blade glittered with reflected light from the parking area despite its dried, brown blood stains.

Euphoria swelled within her.

But also a nagging feeling: The knife should be placed in its case where it belonged. It shouldn't be lying loose in an envelope.

She rested the dagger on her lap, opened the second envelope, and removed a case with leather so old it looked cracked like a shattered window.

The dagger grew warmer in her lap, but that didn't seem strange to her. She snapped open the case. The inside was covered in velvet with a cut-out that matched the shape of the blade, cross-guard, and handle. She grasped the handle, and it was as if a magnetic force pulled the dagger toward the case. It belonged there. It needed to be there. And seemingly on its own, the dagger slipped into the cut-out.

Another wave of euphoria swept through Lepore, growing stronger and stronger. Such feelings never last if you're lucky enough to have them. Hers went on and on.

Holding the case in both hands, she raised it to eye level. The metal gleamed with reflected ambient light, as if showing approval of her.

At that moment, a tiny voice from deep inside her scolded

her for handling the evidence like this, corrupting it. Why had she done that?

"I don't care," she said aloud.

Nothing mattered other than this euphoria.

Nothing mattered other than the power surging through her hands from the dagger case, moving up through her arms, into her chest, and up her neck to her head.

Nothing mattered other than following the commands in her head that blotted out all other sounds.

The commands told her what she must do. And she was happy to. Because nothing mattered other than this sublime euphoria.

With the dagger in its case upon her lap, she merged onto the highway, but took the next exit, crossed under the highway, and merged again headed southbound.

The dagger never made it to the FBI crime lab.

CHAPTER 19

ON THE ROAD TO SAN MARCOS

I should have notified Samson and Lepore about what I was doing. But I followed the supernatural, intuitive path, and they followed the empirical. Sometimes, our paths needed to go their separate ways. So I stood on the upper deck of the municipal parking garage next to the visitors' center, where many of San Marcos' tourists parked. The Simpsons' crossover SUV sat by itself, its black finish splattered with the white of bird droppings, like a pigeon and seagull expressionistic painting.

I had the vehicle's license plate number from the couple's room registration record. I had a spare set of keys that I had found in Dennis' suitcase. When they had checked in, I suggested choosing a municipal lot, and said I would reimburse the charges when they checked out. To get here, I had to pace through almost all the city's lots. I began with the one nearest the inn, which I had recommended. Of course, their car wasn't there. So I methodically made my way through each facility, small and large, walking along each row, searching for a Georgia plate with their number, pressing the key fob to make things easier. So here I was, at the lot farthest from the inn.

I didn't even want to guess how high the parking fee would be, after all the time the vehicle had sat here.

I unlocked the car. I hoped Dennis had driven here from Athens, since the leather-wrapped steering wheel would be a good receptacle of memories. If he hadn't, I hoped he had gripped the armrest on the passenger-seat door.

I climbed into the driver's seat. The car smelled of peppermint. The seat was pushed way back to accommodate a tall driver like Dennis. That was a good sign. I lightly traced my fingertips on the wheel. I sensed plenty of psychic energy in it. Steering wheels are always dependable that way.

I grasped the wheel lightly with my right hand, trying to avoid being sucked into a powerful memory. I needed to assess what was here. It was like scanning the index of a book. This was the technique Laurel had taught me, to avoid randomly plunging into dangerous or violent memories. To establish at least some degree of control over my strange gift.

I skimmed over the boring minutia of driving directions, gas refills, parking instructions. The car was only a couple of years old, so the memories weren't excessive. I moved closer to the present. The easiest place to start would be the couple's hours-long drive to San Marcos.

Taking a deep breath, I tightly gripped the wheel with both hands and—

—freaking jerk cut me off! Boy, I got to calm down. Too edgy. It's like I miss having the dagger in my hand. It makes me feel so good. That's weird, but it's true. In the suitcase in the back of the car is where it belongs now. Can't exactly drive safely when I'm blissing out, can I? And Monique would ask why I've got an ancient leather case in my lap. I don't even know why I brought it with me on this trip. I should have

kept it in its hiding place at home, but I was just compelled to bring it. It was the right thing to do. I would have felt unprepared without it, like I was missing something. I would have been anxious all weekend, and that would have ruined things between Monique and me . . .

It's weird how I felt destined to have the dagger. When Bobby showed me the stuff, I took one look at the dagger and knew I had to have it. Couldn't care less about the gold and silver coins. The dagger grabbed my eyes and sang to me. And I was bothered so much that it wasn't in its case. Weird, but I knew it belonged there, and things weren't right when they were separated. I saw a photo of the museum, and they were displayed separately. That was true for years. And it was wrong, so wrong. The life was draining from the dagger while it sat exposed, alone . . .

As soon as I got my hands on the dagger—and boy, it felt good in my hands—I put it back in its case and absorbed the head-rush of pleasure. Like it was thanking me for doing the right thing. All was right in the world again, and I was blissing out as I held the case with the dagger in it. That's got to be the cheapest drug trip you can get. Well, cheap, if you don't count the ten grand I paid Bobby for it! But it was money well spent . . . there will come a time when the dagger should be removed. And once it's removed, it must be used. Once it's used, it must be returned to the case so it can reenergize and be directed to future assignments. I don't know how I know this, but I just do.

How will I know when it's time to use the dagger? And what will I use it for? I hope I will be told. I believe I will be. I swear, this dagger is magical. It must be something about where it was found, that Spanish Inquisition torture room. Was the dagger used to torture heretics, or did it belong to one, and the Inquisition confiscated it? I don't know, but the thing seems holy to me. Like a saint's relic that can heal you. Can a dagger heal? Seems like a strange thing for a dagger to do. But when I'm holding it, I feel healed. I'm full of happiness, energy, and strength. I feel like the most powerful guy in the world. So I guess it is magical, right? It's nuts.

That thing could be worth millions of dollars, but I would never part with it. Never, ever.

I'd have it here with me in my lap if I could. If it didn't make me lose concentration for driving. And didn't make me look like a weirdo in Monique's eyes. She almost caught me the other night when I snuck out to the garage to hold the dagger case. Like I was a naughty teenager! I should stop thinking about it. I'm craving it now like a drug addict. I've got to concentrate on the road—

—I jumped out of the memory as its intensity and emotion faded.

Wow, that was weird. Just from what Laurel and I experienced from the case, it was clear the dagger had great power. But I had imagined nothing like this.

It occurred to me how strongly I wanted to give the case to the police. I had thought I was just doing the right thing. And I also wanted it far from me. But was there some energy or power in it that made me unite it with the dagger? If that was true, it was unsettling to know I'd been manipulated like that.

Now that I knew how powerful the dagger was, I could almost believe it could compel someone to use it against someone else. Based on his thoughts, I believed Dennis was headed in that direction. It was as if he were waiting for his orders.

Still, who used it against his wife? Dennis couldn't have, because he was dead. Her removing it from its case must have caused a problem.

The thought crept into my head: Could Monique have been influenced to use the dagger to kill herself?

No, there's no way she could have done so much damage to her own body, right? She would have lost consciousness too quickly to butcher herself like that.

Simpson's thoughts were, once the dagger is removed from

its case, "it must be used. Once it's used, it must be returned to the case." He also described the surge of power he felt when he put it back in the case.

Maybe it hadn't been such a good idea to give the case to the police. Now that the dagger had been used on Monique, it was most likely neutralized. If the police put it back into its case . . . what would happen then?

I called Detective Lepore. She didn't answer.

"Hi Detective, this is Darla Chesswick. Just wanted you to know it's probably not a good idea to put the dagger in that case I brought you. Call me and I'll explain."

I didn't know how I could explain without bringing the supernatural into it.

I called Samson. At least he understood the supernatural, as much as he pretended otherwise.

"Samson," he answered.

"Hi, it's Darla. I tried reaching Detective Lepore, but she didn't pick up."

"Yeah?" he asked impatiently.

"It's a long story, but you should know that I found a case in the room of the Simpsons. The case was for the dagger that killed Mrs. Simpson. I gave it to Detective Lepore to put into evidence."

"I know."

"Well, make sure that no one puts the dagger into the case."

"Why?"

"There's magic involved. Dangerous magic. I'm not sure I fully understand yet."

"It just so happens that Cynthia is taking the dagger to the FBI crime lab in Jacksonville for additional tests," Samson said. "I don't know if she brought the case, too, but it should be packaged separately from the dagger."

"Good."

"I'll tell her as soon as she calls me back."

"You can't get through to her either?"

"Um, not at the moment."

That wasn't good. But I didn't say so.

A thought occurred to me. "When Dennis Simpson was killed, did you check to see if he had a criminal record?"

"Yeah. Hang on, let me check." The clicking of a keyboard came over the phone. "He has two priors: trafficking in stolen goods."

"Thanks. Please let me know if you learn anything new," I said.

He agreed and hung up. I locked the Simpsons' car and drove home in mine.

Thoughts about the dagger kept nagging me. I needed to know more about its story before it was stolen from the treasure museum and sold to Dennis.

From the photos I had seen, the dagger and case were separated when on display. Shouldn't this have caused a problem?

I went on the internet and searched for Jules Monsignor's Treasure Museum, but more thoroughly than I had the first time. When I learned the date it opened, I searched prior to that, but I found mostly public relations fluff about exciting plans to open a new museum and tourist draw.

Next, I switched to the website of our local newspaper which had a good searchable archive of their articles.

Then, I found it.

"Museum employee slain in gruesome knife attack. Martin Scalloway, 28, was found murdered by multiple stab wounds Tuesday morning at the site of the new Jules Monsignor's Treasure Museum in San Marcos. The body of the curation coordinator was found by employees arriving for the day, who said Scalloway had worked late the previous night installing artifacts in display cases. Police say there is no evidence of forced entry into the building, which will open to the public next month. Police say they have no suspects and encourage the public to call with any tips."

I avoided the dance of trying to call Lepore first, so I called Samson directly.

"Can you please take a look at this murder?" I asked after paraphrasing the article. "Lepore confirmed the dagger she found in my inn was stolen from the museum. I'm curious if it was the same dagger used in this murder."

"If it was the same weapon, our system should have flagged it. But I'll check it out. Let me call you back."

I went about my daily routine at the inn, preparing and serving afternoon tea with Julie's help. But my mind was fixated on the dagger. Finally, Samson called.

"You're amazing," Samson said.

"What do you mean? Though, of course, I agree."

"The murder at the museum was just like Monique Simpson's. No physical evidence of another person. No signs of a struggle. Only the victim's prints found on the knife. All signs would point toward suicide, except the wounds to the victim. They were too massive to have come from a suicide."

"What does the file say about the murder weapon?"

"Based on the description, it sounds like the same dagger. The problem was, it was labeled as a 'Renaissance-era dagger' in the museum murder, and as an 'antique knife' in the recent murder. So there wasn't a match when we searched for it."

"So how did the museum get it back after their employee was killed?" I asked.

"Well, oddly enough, it looks like the murder was deemed a suicide in the end. At times, there's a lot of pressure to close cases, lowering the number of cold cases we have. I bet that was what happened. The owner of the museum demanded the dagger back, and we had no reason, anymore, to keep it as evidence."

"So, it was delivered to the museum and placed in the glass display where it couldn't harm anyone, even though it wasn't in its case," I thought out loud.

"What are you talking about?"

It was time to share everything I knew with Samson.

"This is going to sound strange, and you don't have to believe it," I said. "But this is my theory of the dagger, based on the memories I've read."

I explained the dagger contained large amounts of black magic, or was possessed by a malevolent spirit. The dagger must always be in its case; removing the dagger from its case and separating them would lead to your death from the dagger. Your death would be by your own hand, but your hand would be controlled by the magic or malevolent force. The only time you are permitted to remove the dagger would be when commanded to kill someone.

Once the dagger is used on someone, it influences the bearer to return it to its case. If not, the dagger loses power and becomes neutralized. The museum curator died because he removed the dagger from the case. When it was returned to the museum, it was displayed separately, but this wasn't a problem. The dagger had satisfied its requirement to kill, but separated from its case, it lost power.

Returning it to its case makes the dagger powerful again. In this state, it can send you on a mission to kill someone, like it did with Dennis. He simply never had the chance to complete his mission.

"Who was Dennis supposed to kill, and who commanded him to do it?" Samson asked.

"I don't know. I guess the evil entity commanded him. Whoever or whatever that is."

"Man, this is bizarre. Where did this dagger come from?"

"An archeological find right here in San Marcos. A crypt was discovered beneath a downtown lot where a colonial building once stood. Some people speculate the crypt was a torture chamber used by the Spanish Inquisition."

"You've got to be kidding me." Samson gave a rueful laugh. "And I'm supposed to explain all of this to Detective Lepore?"

"You can translate it into Cop-ese. The important thing is to tell her to be careful and not to put the dagger in the case."

"Wait a minute. You said when they're separated, you end up disemboweling yourself."

"If you're the one who separated them. Monique separated them, and she paid the price with her own life. Since then, the dagger has probably become dormant or neutralized. If Detective Lepore reunites them, she'll reawaken the power. That's my best guess."

"So how is this dagger connected to the murder attempts against you and your friends?"

"I don't think it is," I said. "I believe it's a coincidence that the husband of the person assigned to kill me had it."

"You said he was meant to kill someone?"

"I'm not positive, but it seemed that way from his thoughts."

"Any idea who the target was?"

"Nope. But I'll check again with the stuff he left in the room. Maybe I can pick up some more memories."

CHAPTER 20

BOLO

The folder was tucked into a pocket on the inside of Dennis Simpson's suitcase. It was a printed-out spreadsheet with notes scrawled on it in pen. I couldn't make sense of it at first.

But, studying it more closely, I saw that most of the columns of text were abbreviations, interspersed with columns of numbers and dates. It appeared to be an inventory list with dates of acquisition and the initials of potential buyers.

From the abbreviations, I managed to make out gold and silver coins, emeralds, swords, pistols, a Michelangelo sketch, a Picasso etching, a pearl-handled pistol, and more priceless items.

Dennis Simpson was a broker of rare art and antiquities. And I would bet a great deal of it was stolen.

Finally, I spotted it:

"15th C. dagger w/gems."

This had to be the dagger in question. It was from the fifteenth century! In the date column was a day from May of this year, which was not long after the treasure museum was looted.

The initials, which I assumed were the name of the buyer, were meaningless to me, but the police could probably find a spreadsheet somewhere that deciphered them.

So, Dennis was approached by the thief who looted the treasure museum. He bought the dagger from the thief, then found a buyer. Presumably, he had been planning to deliver the dagger to the buyer in the near future. That's the impression I received from thought fragments I picked up on the paper.

The printed spreadsheet didn't give up any more secrets. Crouching in the inn's storeroom, I ran my hands over the interior of the suitcase, hoping to pick up useful memories. I didn't have much luck. Packing and unpacking was a rote exercise, and I caught only random thoughts about wrinkled clothing, going through Customs in Hong Kong, dirty laundry.

The outside of the suitcase was even less helpful. If there were any durable memories, they would be on the handles.

When I had packed the suitcase before, I had picked it up by the handle on the end opposite the wheels, and rolled it downstairs using the retractable handle. Nothing had jumped out at me then, but I gave the handles another try.

More scattered thoughts about the logistics of travel. Relief that he found room in a jet's overhead bin. Frustration about a rental car. Pleasant surprise about a hotel room.

I tried to dig deeper. To—

—put it in the car tonight so Monique doesn't inspect my packing and take a look inside. I'll place it in the garage right now—

—and then I picked up quick thoughts after that about Room 303 and doubts that it was actually haunted. So far, I hadn't found any useful information.

I was about to give up, when I noticed the leather handle on the side of the suitcase. A handle you would only use when sticking the suitcase into a space or pulling it out. I wrapped my hand around the leather and—

—ah, the ecstasy of touching the dagger case when I slipped it inside here . . . I am so honored that He has chosen me to use his tongue of fire to smite his enemy: the woman who fooled him, ensnared him, forced him to lend His power to her own ends. He will not be a tool of a mere mortal, and I shall prove to her how mortal she is. I shall cut out her heart with His tongue of fire and I shall show it to her before she expires, so her last thought on earth is how foolish she was to ensnare Him with her sorcery . . .

How will I know her? He will show me. He has directed me to the place, and, when I see her face, I shall know that she is the one. And He will tell me when to act, and where, but I already know how. With the Tongue of Fire in my hand, I shall be invincible to her, and when I return it to its case, the ecstasy I will feel shall be beyond my most fevered dreams. And, wait, Monique's coming out here—

—I shuddered after the memory shut off. Boy, I'd never been in the head of a homicidal maniac before. Don't try this at home, folks. I felt not only frightened, but disgusted.

But did I learn anything I could act on? I didn't think so. For a while there, I worried that I was his target and that he had been headed here to kill me like his wife was. But then there was all that weird stuff about ensnaring "Him" with sorcery and using "His" power. I can assure you that I haven't ensnared any evil entities.

And who was the "He" Dennis referred to? Mewling's followers called him the royal "He." Was that who Dennis was thinking about? Or was it the evil entity Laurel and I sensed?

But the dagger had other plans for him while he was in San Marcos.

While he was whining about Monique mixing business with

pleasure on their anniversary trip, he was doing the exact same thing. On the worst anniversary celebration ever.

As an aside, I wondered if Simpson, had he carried out the murder, still would have sold the dagger to the buyer he had lined up. He would have had to clean it up awfully well. But I had a feeling that he was too attached to the weapon and the euphoria it gave him to part with it.

I picked up my phone to call Samson and tell him what I had learned.

He didn't answer. I couldn't leave this information in a voicemail, so I called him again a few minutes later.

"I can't talk right now," he snapped.

"I found some information about Dennis Simpson," I said.

"I've got to go."

"Wait, what's wrong?"

"Detective Lepore is missing."

"What do you mean?"

"The FBI lab said she never showed up, and she hasn't answered any of my calls. No one else's either. We've put out a BOLO alert for her."

"I wonder if this has something to do with the dagger."

"It's just a freaking dagger. What happened to her? I'll call you later."

The line went dead.

Did Lepore put the dagger back in the case? If so, had she become enthralled with it like Simpson?

It was a vexing mystery. Meanwhile, I was no closer to finding out who was ordering the attacks on The Memory Guild. And now, Lepore and Samson had a much bigger priority than my safety. Despite my rough beginnings with Lepore, I sincerely hoped she was all right.

Breakfast at the Esperanza Inn was free, of course, and largely consisted of Continental fare such as fresh bread and baked goods, fruit, juices, tea, and coffee. But I always included French toast or pancakes, and proteins such as an egg casserole, sausages, cold cuts and cheeses. I served them buffet style in chafing dishes, and spent the morning rushing back and forth from the breakfast room to the kitchen as guests straggled in. The breakfast room was warm and inviting, with a view of the courtyard and the gardens in it. Though it was a buffet, breakfast at the Esperanza Inn was a far cry from the frenzied scenes at the chain-hotel free breakfasts.

This was my hardest task of each day. Afternoon tea was much easier. In between those events, I ran around the inn responding to the endless requests and crises, rarely having enough time to handle the ongoing renovations.

Now, it was a complaint about a leaky sink in 301 that got my attention. I'm not particularly handy, but my years as an innkeeper have taught me to always try to fix something yourself before you bring in a contractor. In small inns and hotels, our margins are too thin to mess with. I wasn't big enough to justify hiring a full-time maintenance person. I had to depend upon myself and the housekeepers to keep this ship afloat.

At my bed-and-breakfast in Key West, I had a husband to help me. You've already heard how that turned out.

Julie's cart was parked in front of 302 while she was inside cleaning. I had to squeeze past it. It needed to be closer to the hallway wall. I grabbed the handle to push—

—and he looks down at me in bed, his gray eyes that were once so warm and caring, now stone-cold. The lovemaking had been good, though he had seemed distant. And now I can see in his eyes that he is

ready to move on from me. His career is taking off in a new direction, and he is actually making more money than before. With even more fanatical followers who seem younger and younger, and with more and more goggle-eyed girls adoring him. I—

—yanked my hand from the handle and staggered past the cart before Julie could see me and the look on my face.

I had seen, through Julie's eyes, the face of Lance Mewling.

CHAPTER 21
EVEN HER TAX FORM

I didn't have a proper office at the inn. I kept a filing cabinet in the kitchen for invoices and receipts. My guest records were stored digitally. Everything else was kept in cardboard boxes in the guest house where I lived. That included the meager files I kept for personnel.

Two housekeepers barely warranted the term "personnel."

Julie's file was where I began to research her and see if I could find out why she had an intimate memory of Lance Mewling. The file wasn't very useful. There was only her address and contact information, plus her W-4. There was no resume or record of previous employment. From what I remembered, I had run an ad for a housekeeper, and she had emailed me back, claiming she had worked at a few local bed-and-breakfasts. When I interviewed her, she added she had originally been in academia. I simply took her for her word. I didn't ask for references, because I didn't have time to check them. I figured, just let her work and if she does a good job, keep her on. Once I got to know her, she told me she'd been in the academic world, but she didn't elaborate.

There's no Human Resources department at your typical mom-and-pop inn. Or, in my case, mom without the pop.

Next, I did what anyone else would do, search the internet. The internet makes you feel as if you have all the information in the world at your fingertips, but that's totally wrong. You only have the information that's been digitalized and not hidden behind a firewall. And you have algorithms feeding you the information they think you want, instead of what you really need. That's how people like Mewling's followers plunge into the rabbit holes of conspiracy theories.

Anyway, I searched and searched for Julie Fodder. I found zilch. There were sites that promised me all sorts of information about her for a fee, which I ignored. She seemed to have no online records, no social media. She had left no digital footprint at all.

I searched for her name plus Lance Mewling, and nothing useful came up. Next, I tried Lance Mewling plus "Julie." I got some Julies, but no Julie Fodder. I clicked on some of these, hoping she had a maiden name or married name that wasn't Fodder. Most of the hits were references or photos on online gossip sites. The one that had the most results was called *The Eye*. They published a lot of photos of Mewling. I went to their main site and searched only for Lance Mewling.

Boy, they sure had an obsession with the man. There were lots of paparazzi shots of him and his various wives showing up at society events. I found plenty of stories gloating over his firing from the television station, and about his growing number of fanatic followers.

Then, I stumbled upon the photo.

The shot was of Mewling leaving a restaurant with Julie.

Except her name in the caption wasn't Julie. It was Jane Whistler. She was identified as Mewling's researcher and assistant at the television station.

The woman I had hired to clean the rooms of my inn had given me a fake name. And I had been too lazy to check her background. Even her W-4 form had Julie Fodder on it.

Using her real name, my searches yielded plenty of fruit.

She had worked for Mewling for years, not just at the station, but also helping him research his books and newspaper columns. There was some speculation that Jane Whistler was a contributing factor in the collapse of one of Mewling's marriages.

When Mewling was fired from the television station because of his Holocaust denialism, Whistler was fired, too. After that, I found no more mentions of her.

Interesting. The Memory Guild's campaign against Mewling had harmed Jane Whistler, as well. A search of the county's public records showed Whistler had lost her house to foreclosure not long afterward.

The weakness of my theory, that The Memory Guild had been targeted because of its campaign against Mewling, was the fact that the Guild was secret. Mewling might have gone after Noordlun, the public face of the campaign, but how would he have known about the other members of the Guild?

I came across a connection that could possibly explain that. I discovered Whistler had been a graduate student in the San Marcos College Department of History. The department that Dr. Noordlun chaired.

I refused to wait until the Guild convened a meeting. I needed to speak to Dr. Noordlun right away. It took three phone calls to his assistant before I got an appointment with the professor the next morning.

In the meantime, I acted like nothing had changed whenever I spoke to the woman I formerly knew as Julie. My resentment remained concealed.

Dr. Sven Noordlun could pass as a Viking chieftain. The tall man, with long white hair and a bushy white beard, had a forceful presence that commanded the respect of The Memory Guild and, undoubtedly, entire lecture halls of students.

I sat across the desk from him in his office, crammed with books in tall, ornately carved dark-wood bookcases. He stared at me intently, as I reviewed all I had learned.

Putting his elbows on the desk, he rested his face in his hands.

"Why did I not think of Jane Whistler?" he asked himself regretfully. "I didn't know she worked for Mewling and had a romantic relationship with him. It makes so much more sense now."

"What can you tell me about her?"

"She was a graduate student here, sharing my specialization in the early colonial history of the Americas. She became my teaching assistant. I relied so much on her, I'm afraid I let my guard down. I knew she admired me, but I didn't realize how obsessive she was. Somehow, she found out about the Guild."

Well, that explained a lot.

"She asked if she could join the Guild," Noordlun continued. "I was quite taken aback, both by her knowledge of the Guild and her desire to join it."

"How did she find out our names?"

"I suppose by eavesdropping on me and reading my correspondence. It angered me. In any event, I explained we only accept members with paranormal or supernatural abilities. She countered by pointing out that I didn't have those abilities, and she believed her historical expertise was enough of a contribution. I disagreed. And I explained I was the exception because I founded the Guild in the first place."

"How did she react?" I asked.

"Reasonably well, at first. But over time, she repeated her request. More insistently. Then, it took a dark turn."

"What do you mean?"

"She said she had something to offer other than paranormal abilities. She had been learning magic. Unfortunately, it was black magic, taught to her by a sorceress who had been banned by the Magic Guild."

"She could do magic, for real?"

"So she claimed. I continued to refuse her request, and she quit as my teaching assistant. I never saw her or heard of her again after she received her doctorate."

"Obviously, she left academia," I said. Then an idea occurred to me. "This might sound crazy, but after Jane was hired by Mewling, his career took off."

"I think you're giving her too much credit. She wasn't that good of an assistant."

"But maybe she helped Mewling in additional ways. From what I've read, he went from a mildly popular local commentator to a nationally known figure with a syndicated talk show. But what's really astounding is how quickly his fan base grew. His number of followers exploded, especially online. Extremely devoted fans."

"Yes. I suppose the internet is strange that way."

"What if her magic had something to do with it?"

Dr. Noordlun appeared startled.

"What if she conjured powers that gave Mewling's words

exceptional power of persuasion?" I asked. "What if she essentially helped Mewling brainwash his audience?"

"I have no expertise in black magic, but in theory there might be a way to do that."

"Mewling's followers aren't just rabid fans. They'd do anything he told them to. Maybe even murder people. People like us. But it was Jane Whistler who actually ordered them to do it."

"If Jane lost her job when Mewling was fired, I could see her resenting me," Noordlun said. "And she must have assumed the Guild was working with me."

"Right. She not only lost her livelihood and had to take jobs as a housekeeper. She lost her career because of the same organization that rejected her when she wanted to join."

Noordlun nodded. "But wouldn't Mewling continue to pay her? He's obviously doing quite well in the second act of his career."

"I guess not. I think they continued to have an affair, but maybe he believed he didn't need her services anymore. He was super popular. And he didn't need a researcher anymore, because he peddled only untruths and conspiracy theories. An intern would be all he needed."

"Nevertheless, he could afford to still pay her."

"Unless he was put off by the black magic," I said.

"Do you believe she's the one behind the attempts on us?"

"The more I think about it, the more I believe it. I recently asked Mewling for an autograph, and I asked him to make it out to The Memory Guild. It was obvious by his reaction he had never heard of the Guild. Whistler, though, has a motive to harm us."

"Yes." He frowned. "And who are these assassins?"

"Mewling's followers, of course. She used her powers to

compel them to attack us. I don't know if she persuaded specific individuals or enchanted a large number, hoping that some would respond. Remember, these guys didn't act like professional killers. For the most part, they're incompetent amateurs."

Although some did come awfully close to succeeding, I thought.

"It seems farfetched that she could enchant people over the internet," Noordlun said.

"Why not? The internet has become such an important way to communicate and absorb information. For some people, it's their primary way. If you can cast a spell on someone out of your visual range, you can do it over the internet, as well."

"The obvious question is how do we stop her? I think it's futile to expect to convince the police she's using black magic to enact assassinations."

"Yeah. But maybe they can tie her to the killers through her digital communications."

"Perhaps. But what will you do with this woman working in your inn? Will you confront her, or fire her?"

"Eventually. For now, I'll keep an eye on her. I don't know if it was a coincidence that she ended up working for me, or if it was a way to be close to the Guild. But I'll try to use it to my advantage."

"If she truly has these magical powers, the police might not be able to stop her. Even if they do, she can still harm us greatly. How can we fight someone who has magic?"

"Good question," I said.

"I will notify the Magic Guild that a black magician is operating in the city. Hopefully, they can put an end to it."

I agreed it was the best course of action. And after I left, I contacted the one person I knew who understood witchcraft more than my mother. My cousin, Missy.

"OH, MY," SHE SAID OVER THE PHONE. "YOU SHOULD HAVE told me as soon as you realized you were in danger."

"I didn't want to get you involved. You've already been in danger because of me."

I referred to the time she helped rescue Sophie from a clan of vampires in the city where Missy lived. And as if that weren't enough, the time she helped me in San Marcos by battling another foe who used black magic.

"What's the best way to neutralize her magic?" I asked.

"You must understand powerful black magic doesn't harness the energies of the earth like mine does. It relies on demons and other dark forces to do the hard work."

"Uh-oh. That sounds scary."

"It is. For the victims of black magic and for the magicians, too. They're basically riding on the backs of tigers. If they're not careful, the tiger will get them, too."

"That's not exactly comforting."

I explained about the dagger. "Could that be involved?"

"You said this Dennis character was thinking he was on a mission to kill whoever 'ensnared' the entity that controlled him?"

"Basically, yes."

"It sounds as if the tiger wants to get the magician off its back. I'm coming up there to help you."

"No, please. You don't need to get involved in this."

"I should have gotten involved long ago," Missy said.

"Give me more time to look into this. Then, I'll call you."

CHAPTER 22

A DOWNSIDE OF SMOKING

I thought about my conversation with Dr. Noordlun and the financial situation of Julie—I mean, Jane Whistler. Losing your career and being made nearly destitute gave her more of a motive to get revenge. But why was she destitute if Mewling was doing so well? Was he just that much of a jerk?

To me, he seemed like a jerk. I could see him keeping her around only as a mistress, dangling cash to keep her committed but becoming more miserly with it. That kind of cruel treatment would push Whistler into dangerous behavior.

In her mind, the Guild had wronged her by wronging Mewling. But the revenge she sought was only for her.

And as for Mewling, I wondered if his death was really a heart attack. The last time I asked Samson about it, he said they were still waiting for the toxicity report from the medical examiner.

I wanted to find out more about Whistler. Not being a cop, I could think of only two ways.

For the first, I called Diego and asked him to hack into Whistler's email account.

"I will try," he said, "but I need to know the correct email address. I can search for her addresses, but the information you want is probably sent only through a non-public address."

Which leads me to my second way of getting information: telepathy or psychometry. The former hadn't worked on her. Besides, who comes to work and thinks about their private email address? I needed to read more of her memories. Even if I couldn't get the email address, I could learn other valuable information.

While I was pulling a sheet of scones from the oven to be served at afternoon tea, Julie—I mean, Whistler—poked her head in the kitchen.

"I finished all the rooms," she said. "I'm going to afternoon Mass, unless you need help with tea."

"No, I'm good. I didn't know you're a Catholic."

"I am. I go to the cathedral on the city square."

"Such a beautiful place. Well, see you tomorrow."

"Goodnight," she said with a smile that seemed genuine. But this woman, I had learned, was a good actor.

I hadn't picked up any of her thoughts. So, as soon as I heard the door slam, I walked over and put my hand on the spot of the wall where hers had been when she leaned against it just now. There should be just a little—

—I hope she doesn't want me to do her work while she plays detective tonight. The stupid cow—

—and that was it. And it confirmed my opinion: She had a great fake smile.

The reference to the cathedral stuck with me. Didn't Dennis have a memory of anticipating going to the cathedral? It was an interesting coincidence.

As soon as I had made a pass through the breakfast room with the tea cart, I parked it by the entrance and headed to the room where the housekeeping cart was kept. The space, which faced the alley, looked like it had once been a garage in the early days of automobiles, but it had been finished and now housed the washers and dryers, as well as the linens, paper products, a workbench, and spare parts for all the things that seemed to break every day.

This afternoon, it was dimly lit with light coming in the dirty windows facing the alley. On the wall near the washers was a small table with two chairs, a microwave, and a coffeemaker. I always had hot coffee in the kitchen, and the housekeepers were welcome to it, but I guessed it was easier to grab their own back here during a break or while waiting for towels to dry.

I touched the handle of the coffeemaker. It held random thoughts from Bella, but nothing coherent from Whistler. In the work sink was a dirty mug, but it, too, only had Bella's thoughts. I glanced around the large room, trying to imagine Whistler's routine here. Aside from the cart, most of the items she would handle only briefly.

I turned on the overhead lights. The switch box, on an unfinished wall next to the door to the alley, protruded from a stud. A disposable cigarette lighter sat atop it.

I never saw my housekeepers smoke, but, come to think of it, I remembered smelling cigarettes on Whistler before. I picked up the lighter—

—the scratch of the wheel, burst of flame, the nutty smell of paper and tobacco on the first puff from the cigarette . . . I need to check my phone (putting lighter down)—

—too brief to get anything useful from the lighter.

I opened the door and looked at the old, cracked asphalt. Sure enough, there were cigarette butts littering the ground.

Normally, this litter would anger me, but now it could be useful. People do a lot of thinking when they stand outside smoking.

I squatted, and, yuck, picked up the four squashed butts lying near the door.

I brought them inside, placed them on the break table, and sat beside it. I held one of the smelly butts in my fingers and—

—the lawyer still hasn't returned my calls. I know Lance put me in his will. He even showed me a copy. So why isn't the lawyer calling? Is there a problem? I wouldn't put it past Lance to revise the will and leave me out of it. But after all I've done for him, how could he do that? It's just one thing after another going wrong for me, ever since those pretentious pricks went after Lance and got him fired. The stuff he said was none of their business. He has an audience that wants to hear arguments bashing the people who are hurting America, so that's what Lance gives to them. It's all true. I don't care what the stupid Memory Guild says.

And how I ended up working for one of those nuts is just another example of how bad my luck is. I have to see her every day! And none of those morons have killed her yet! How incompetent can they be? I should just kill her myself, but that's so beneath me. Okay, the dryer is done. (Tamping out butt.)—

--My eyes opened. I was slouching in the chair. The cigarette butt had fallen from my fingers to the floor.

I had to admit it was weird being in someone's head while they're thinking about wanting your death. Normally, it's good when you can see the world through others' eyes. This was the exception. But at least, it gave me some insight into this woman's twisted mind.

I steeled myself and picked up a second butt. Immediately, I was pulled toward a strong memory, but I resisted being immersed in it. It was a memory, or fantasy, of making love with Mewling. This woman was truly smitten with the man. I would grant that he was charismatic—millions of his followers would agree with that—but I found nothing at all sexy about him. I pushed away the memory and tossed the butt into the trash.

Now for the third butt. It had a smear of lipstick on it. I held it and—

—checked my email on my phone. Here's one from Barkin . . . (scroll through the thread) . . . says he doesn't know what happened to Spade. No one has heard from him, no record of him at the jail. He must have bailed on us. Okay, good, Barkin says he will do the job on the wheelchair lady on Friday. Good. It's amazing how obedient these guys are after I use the spell. They sound perfectly coherent, not in a zombie trance. But anything I ask them to do, they immediately agree. Maybe I should have used the spell on Lance . . . okay, back to work—

—I opened my eyes. Did that mean Lauren was in danger? I needed to warn her and tell the police. I held onto the visual image that Whistler had had of her phone screen. The date was yesterday, so Friday meant tomorrow.

I still retained the image of the chain of older emails from Whistler in which her email address was visible in the header. I jotted it down on a message pad before I forgot it.

One more cigarette butt to read. This one was only two-thirds consumed. I sensed it had been smoked quickly, under great anxiety, and I—

—don't know how much longer I can control the Father of Lies. He resists me now, every time I summon him when casting the spell. The spell is so effective because this demon is freaking powerful—more than I first realized. I only thought I'd need to summon him once or twice, but the assassins keep failing. And the way the demon threatened me last night . . . he hates me for controlling him, and I'm surprised I can. But not much longer. I have to stop before he kills me. Yes, I don't need to do this anymore—

—my heart was pounding. I was experiencing her worry and fear. And she had fragmentary images of the summoning and the glowing red eyes in the darkness. She was messing with a seriously powerful dark force.

Like Missy said, Whistler was riding on the back of a tiger. And it was ready to eat her.

I threw the cigarette butts away and walked over to the cleaning cart, parked near the washing machines and the shelves of bed linens and towels. This was why I had come to this room in the first place.

I placed both hands on the rubber-coated handlebar. There were lots of memories accumulated here, including Bella's. They would be difficult to sort out.

I used the technique Laurel had taught me of skimming across the memories. A lot of them were mundane work-related thoughts about to-do lists and frustrations, about nasty messes and stained sheets, stolen towels and broken vacuums. Whistler left the residue of anger and hatred. I couldn't imagine going through life like that, blaming others for everything wrong with your life. But she did. And look where it got her. She was conspiring to murder innocent strangers and practicing black magic to do it.

I came across a strong, recent—

—he's dead, dead, dead! It was his fault he died. He should have known he was pushing me too far—taking advantage of me, using me without a second thought, throwing me away when he was done with me like the dirty tissues I have to empty from wastebaskets every day. I wish he could have died more painfully. I would have ordered one of his brain-dead followers to do it, but they're so brainwashed they would never harm the god they worship.

I should have gotten the Father of Lies to kill him. Give him a taste of the dangerous evil I had to deal with on his behalf. He thought it was just a simple spell to make his words more persuasive to his infantile audience, but I told him what the spell involved and how dangerous it was to use a demon's power. But, no, Lance didn't care about the risks I was taking. He just wanted his ratings to soar and the sponsors to pay more for the higher ratings. He just wanted the internet hits, the video views, the fame and attention and the money the money the money. So much money. He didn't care when he got himself fired.

But what about me? He never helped me, except for the paltry hand-outs I had to earn on my back. And when I told him I was going after the jerks who got us fired, and how I was doing it, he got scared. "No, you can't do that," he said. "You can't murder anyone." And when I reminded him I wasn't doing the killing, he's like, "no, no, you can't make my followers murder people. It will make me look bad." Well, you already look bad to anyone who's not a conspiracy nut, so why do you care? I'm the one who has to handle a freaking demon.

And that look in his eyes—like he thought I was crazy! He was actu-ally afraid of me! The one who kissed his butt and helped make him famous! He wanted nothing more to do with me, so I got the last word. Yeah, I gave him what he deserved. He's dead, dead, dead, and I will not shed a tear for that pig . . . but if he had only given me a kind word in the end—

—the memory trailed off with an image of Whistler leaving the cart in this room.

I was shaken, having been in her disturbed mind. But now I had some explanations for why all this craziness had happened. And crazy it was. If someone told me this story, I wouldn't believe it. But I had lived through it and was lucky to have survived.

Knock on wood. I couldn't be certain about the surviving part until Whistler was in jail.

I hoped Lepore was okay. And that she and Samson could focus on this case again. Now, at least, I had information to work with.

I wanted to fire Whistler immediately, but didn't want her to skip town. If we could get the proper evidence, it would be easier to arrest her if the police knew she'd be here at the inn.

As soon as night fell, I would contact Diego and give him the email address that Whistler used for plotting the murders. And, out of curiosity and concern, I sought to learn about the Father of Lies.

In the meantime, I had to warn Laurel that an attempt might be made on her life tomorrow.

CHAPTER 23

I'M A MAN IN DISTRESS

I called Laurel to warn her of the danger she was in, but she didn't answer. I left a message telling her she'd been targeted by a person named Barkin, and he was coming tomorrow.

"Please, Laurel, stay here at the inn," I added. "Please. It will be much safer here. He surely knows where you live."

When I didn't hear back from her, I decided to drive to her house. And if she wasn't there, I would go to every place I thought I might find her, from the grocery store to her favorite cafe.

Night had fallen when I reached her house. The neighborhood was idyllic during the day, but at night, the streets that ran perpendicular to the beach had no streetlights and were dark beneath the trees.

I was relieved to see her car in the driveway, and I parked behind it. Lights were on inside the house, so I ran up the stairs, crossed the covered porch, and knocked on the front door.

No answer. I knocked some more. Still, nothing.

"Laurel, are you home?"

It was silent inside. My stomach sank when I considered the possibility the killer had shown up a day early. Was Laurel injured or dead in there?

Or maybe the killer was there now, waiting for me to leave.

I tried the door, but it was locked. I paced the wrap-around porch, peering in windows. Nothing inside seemed suspicious or out of place. All the windows were closed and locked, so I couldn't get in without breaking one of them.

The porch didn't extend to her bedroom window, though, so I couldn't see inside that room. I hoped she wasn't incapacitated in there.

I pounded on the front door again.

"Laurel, are you in there? Are you okay?"

"I'm fine," she said.

I snapped my head around. Laurel was at the bottom of the wheelchair ramp in the front of the house. She sat on her "dune buggy," the wheelchair with the fat tires for traversing sand.

"I just took a roll on the beach," she said. "It's nice and deserted now that the sun went down."

She grabbed the push rims and propelled herself up the ramp.

"Let me help you," I said.

"No thanks. I do this every day, and need to keep my arms strong."

"Did you get my message?" I asked when she arrived on the porch.

"No, sorry. The surf was so loud on the beach, I didn't hear the phone ring."

"From now on, you need to make sure you can."

I explained to her about Whistler's memories I had read and the reference to killing "the wheelchair lady" tomorrow.

"You shouldn't be here by yourself," I said. "Please stay at the inn."

"I suppose that would be a good idea."

"Beginning tonight," I said. "Who knows when he'll show up? I'm not leaving here until you come with me."

"Okay, but I had a recipe I was planning to--"

As if to punctuate what I had said, a loud thump came from the roof on the rear of the house.

"That was too big to be a raccoon," I said.

Heavy footsteps plodded across the cedar-shake roof. They thumped up the roof to the peak, and then down the slope toward the porch where we were.

Not a raccoon, definitely a human.

"Um, you didn't ask a roofing company for an estimate, did you?"

She shook her head, eyes wide with fear.

The heavy man thudded down the roof and onto the porch roof. He was right above us. I was paralyzed with fear.

Wood creaked over my head, just a couple of feet to my left.

The wood snapped.

And two legs plunged through the ceiling, followed by a rain of debris. The legs jolted as the man's hips jammed into the hole, stopping his fall.

Something small and heavy landed on the roof next to him and slid noisily down the shingles to the edge of the roof.

A pistol dropped past us and landed on the sand below.

So a man was hanging from the porch ceiling from the waist to his boots. Is that normal?

"Dang it," said a voice from the roof.

Laurel and I remained frozen as the man struggled to free himself, his legs kicking, drywall dust falling, but he wasn't going anywhere. He was stuck.

"These have to be the most incompetent assassins the world has ever known," I said.

Maybe it was because of our buildup of fear, but Laurel and I both broke out in laughter.

"Hey, it ain't nice to laugh at me," the voice said above us. "I'm a man in distress."

"What are you doing here?" Laurel called to the ceiling.

"Checking on your roof. I'm a roofer."

Laurel and I exchanged glances.

"Is your name Barkin?" I asked.

"How did you know that?" the man stuck in the roof asked.

"I heard it from the person who assigned you to kill the homeowner."

"I don't know what you're talking about. I just fix roofs."

"With a gun? And that wasn't a nail gun."

"You need personal protection in my line of work. People get upset by how much their roof costs."

"This guy isn't going anywhere," I said at top volume. "I think we should torture him until he tells us the truth. Go get your blowtorch, and we'll start on his feet and work our way up."

"No, no, you gotta be sick in the head or something! I'm a man in distress here."

"I'm going to call the police," I said, "so you'll be helped off the roof. But I want answers first. Before you go to jail."

"I don't have to tell you nothin'."

"Let's start with his left foot."

The legs hanging from the ceiling began kicking wildly. He dropped about an inch deeper, but appeared to be wedged even more firmly now.

"Don't touch me," he wailed.

"The cops will give you a break if you can prove you were

forced to come here to kill my friend," I said. "If you can blame it on duress or threats to your safety."

"They brainwashed me," he whined. "When the lady called me, her voice had a crazy effect on me. She said words in a language I couldn't understand, and then my brain went all mushy. And I promised I'd do what she wanted. Somehow, I knew I had to, or I would be killed."

"Do you know the lady's name?"

"She called herself The Director."

"Tell this story to the police and the D.A., and maybe you'll be okay."

Of course, my promise was worth about as much as this young man's competence.

I pulled my phone from my pocket and called Samson.

THE NEXT MORNING, I STOPPED BY LAUREL'S HOUSE TO CHECK on her. She was fine, at least that was how she behaved. She was expecting a contractor to stop by any minute to give her an esti-mate on repairing her porch roof. This time, it would be a real roofer. So I kissed her on the cheek and left.

As I waited at a red light on my way home, I saw Sophie's car drive through the intersection and enter the road I was travel-ing, the two-lane beach highway.

What was she doing up this way? I wondered.

The light turned green, and I proceeded, soon finding myself behind Sophie's car. There was no mistaking the old hybrid with its quarter panels in different colors and a bumper sticker for a sea turtle rescue center.

I wasn't technically trailing her if I was already going this way, right? But, yes, I was curious where she was headed, with suspicious possibilities popping into my mind and making me feel guiltier with every pop.

Sophie continued north on the beach road, passing condo complexes and fancy beachfront homes. None of the homes were as big as Mewling's, though. I almost lost her when she turned off on the road that led to the state park. I didn't expect that.

I doubted there would be drug dealers or Nigerian princes hanging out in a state park. The rangers frown on both groups.

I slowed down and pulled over when she arrived at the admission gate and paid the fee. If I went into the park, I would be officially following her. I wouldn't be able to deny it.

What the heck. I drove up to the gate. I could blame it on my maternal instincts. My nosy, suspicious, privacy-invading maternal instincts.

I paid the ranger in the booth my entrance fee, then leaned my head toward the window.

"Is this park safe?" I asked.

"Yes, just be sure to lock your car and don't leave any valuables visible."

"I mean, are there other kinds of criminals here?"

"We've never had violence in the years I've worked here. And don't forget, the park closes at sundown."

"Are there drug dealers here?"

"No. We have a ranger who patrols the park."

"If there were any drug dealers, what part of the park would they be in?"

"Are you asking me to help you find drugs?"

"No," I said, embarrassed. "Just making sure a family member doesn't buy any." I closed my window before I said anything else stupid and drove into the park.

The park had a gorgeous beach, miles long with hardly anyone on it, plus camping, picnic areas, trails, and more. It was a sprawling place, and it took me a while to find Sophie's car. It was parked near a boardwalk to the beach. Only one other car was nearby, a Volkswagen. Drug dealers don't drive Volkswagens, right?

There really wasn't a way for me to spy on Sophie if she was on the beach without blowing my cover. But I walked out on the boardwalk that crossed over the sand dunes to see if she was in view.

She wasn't in view in either direction. In fact, no one was, probably because it was a weekday. Sophie hadn't been here long enough to walk too far away to be seen. Not knowing what to do, I sat on a bench next to the stairs that descended to the sand.

I became lulled by watching the lines of waves rolling in, curling, and crashing onto the sand. The gentle roar of the surf made me sleepy.

A noise rose above the sound of the ocean. It was a rustling among the sea oats and plants that grew on the dunes. The sound came from right below me.

A large animal—no, two animals—were crawling around down there.

Dogs weren't allowed to be unleashed in the park. What kind of critter could they be in the daytime? Did feral hogs live so close to the beach?

I heard a voice. Actually, they were feral humans. They emerged from under the boardwalk and came into view.

They were Sophie and a Hispanic woman around her age.

I cleared my throat loudly. Both women looked up.

"Mom. Why are you here?"

"Your car turned onto A1A in front of me. I continued on my

way, and when you turned into the park, I followed you. I was curious why you went to the park."

"You were following me?"

"Only after you pulled out in front of me."

"Did you think I was going to buy drugs, or something?"

I didn't answer.

The Hispanic woman, with dark skin and straight black hair, spoke up.

"Maybe it's okay to tell her."

"Tell me what?" I asked.

"About Gerta," Sophie said. "Gerta is the friend I told you I was helping."

"I don't understand. Where is she?"

"She lives here."

"You mean she's homeless?"

Sophie and her friend exchanged glances.

"No," Sophie said slowly. "Gerta has a home here. Gerta is a beach troll."

I'd heard legends of beach trolls in Northern Florida centuries ago, but thought they were long gone. The creatures are common in Iceland and Scandinavian countries. I assumed they migrated here for the weather just like everybody else does.

"We found Gerta on the beach. She's sick," the other woman explained. "She's recovering, but hasn't been able to hunt to feed herself and her children."

"That's what I needed the money for," Sophie said. "To buy food and stuff for her. Imelda and I," she gestured at her friend, "can't afford it with the money we make at the restaurant."

"What do beach trolls eat?" I asked.

"Lots of fresh fish," Sophie said. "Lots of it. And sea birds. We had to buy pheasant and quail to substitute for seagull and tern."

"And Oreos," Imelda said. "We learned that beach trolls are addicted to Oreos."

"They're not alone in that. So where, exactly, does she live?" I asked.

"Under the boardwalk, of course," Sophie said. "Regular trolls live under bridges. Beach trolls live beneath structures like this."

My exposure to weirdness used to be only my telepathy. Then, I developed my psychometric powers. Which came at the same time I learned vampires and werewolves and living gargoyles were real.

So, beach trolls? Why not?

"Can I meet Gerta?" I asked.

"We have to ask her first," Sophie said.

"She's very friendly," Imelda said. "I'm sure she'll want to meet you."

"Let me know when, and I'll come back here."

CHAPTER 24
THE FATHER OF LIES

The Memory Guild assembled in the domed stone room that might or might not exist. The ten of us were assembled, but not really there, having used astral travel to come to our gathering place, while our physical bodies remained where they had been before. This was way better than video conferencing, except you had to wear pants.

I summarized to the group what I had discovered.

"I take responsibility," Dr. Noordlun said. "I didn't think of Jane Whistler as a possible suspect. Being denied membership in the Guild is not enough of a motive to have people killed. But, when coupled with the damage to her career and her treatment by Mewling, her grievances are much greater."

"Don't blame yourself," Summer said. "You couldn't have known. It's so illogical."

"Thank you, but we almost lost one of our own because of my negligence," Dr. Noordlun said. "Now, we must remedy the situation. Whistler must face justice. And we have a demonic force in our community that must be driven away. I've alerted the other supernatural guilds about its presence."

"It's the Father of Lies," I said.

Everyone stared at me in shock, like I'd burped or something.

"Whistler called the entity the Father of Lies," I said.

"The Father of Lies is the greatest foe of The Memory Guild," Noordlun explained. "In the Bible, Satan was called the Father of Lies, but this isn't Satan. This is a lesser demon, but he is extremely pernicious with an outsized influence on the world today."

"He gives power to lies and misinformation, and helps them spread faster," Laurel explained.

"One of the greatest causes of conflict and misery in humankind is our fear and paranoia caused by beliefs that aren't true," Dr. Noordlun said. "The Father of Lies feeds off that negative energy and amplifies it, unless humans fight back with truth and understanding."

"Whistler used this demon to make Mewling's fans more loyal and to compel some to kill for her?" Diego asked.

"That appears to be the case," Dr. Noordlun said. "Evil people have used the demon's power to cause everything from murders to wars. Many of the darkest moments in human history were made worse by him. He flourished in the ignorance and superstition of the Middle Ages and during the religious persecutions in the centuries that followed. Today, thanks to the internet, we are in another dark age of rumors, false beliefs, and suspicion. The Father of Lies makes conspiracy theories spread like wildfire. He makes people take pleasure in believing what isn't true."

"How do we stop him?" I asked.

"We can't destroy him for good. But we can stamp out his

lies. After all, that's the mission of The Memory Guild. That is our eternal battle. In the short term, however, we have to stop Whistler and make her free the demon from the magic she's using to control him. Then, all we can do is to combat the lies that Mewling has spread and try to discredit his legacy."

"All of us," he continued, "must continue to guard our personal safety until the assassination attempts end. And remain forever vigilant against the lies that are spread around us."

"And on that note, I have some good news for you, Darla," Diego said. "I hacked into Whistler's email account. She has a treasure trove of emails, poorly encrypted, in which she gives explicit orders to assassinate us. I'll share them with you on the other side."

DIEGO WAS RIGHT; HE HAD THE GOODS. I IMMEDIATELY texted Samson and soon got him on the phone. I explained all that I'd learned.

"I have the emails printed and in digital form," I said. "My friend decrypted them."

"That sounds really promising," he said. His voice was anxious and depressed. "The emails might not be enough to convict on their own, but they're enough for an arrest warrant. If we can get one of the would-be assassins to testify against her, she's going away for a long time."

"And Mewling knew about this," I said. "He wasn't directly involved, but allowed it to happen."

"I'm not the least bit surprised."

"Have you heard from Detective Lepore?"

He exhaled deeply. "No. I'm worried she's been hurt. Or your crazy theory about a demon isn't so crazy. Law enforcement is looking for her in both counties. I've been glued to my phone, praying to hear from her."

I was afraid for Lepore, too, but I couldn't help feeling a little sad about how upset Samson was. It went far beyond a professional concern for a colleague. I recognized my feelings of jealousy, and I hated to admit I felt them in a time like this.

"If you want to talk, I'm here for you," I said.

He grunted. Men don't enjoy talking about their feelings, especially if they're in jobs like law enforcement.

"What are Whistler's hours today?" he asked.

"Probably ten to five. I'm pretty easygoing about that if she gets all her work done."

"She might not finish her work today."

"I'll live with it."

CYNTHIA LEPORE DROVE TO SAN MARCOS, FILLED WITH JOY and purpose. Her mission had been revealed to her in startling clarity. It was simple. And it was the right thing to do.

She would free her Father from the magic that bound him and caused him to suffer. He would lend his strength to her so she should not fail. And He would reward her with eternal life and a euphoria even greater than what she'd been feeling from the dagger. A euphoria that lasted every minute of every day, forever.

The dagger would taste the blood it craved. And she would be the guardian of the dagger for all time.

Her Father's dagger. Forged by humans, but imbued with power by her Father centuries ago, after it was used to draw blood from the innocent under the rule of lies. She would keep the dagger close to her forever, and forever share in her Father's power.

The power to defy death, old age, and inconvenient truths. The power to create her own truths. And the power to make others believe in them.

What could be better than that?

And all she had to do was complete one simple task: slay the person who had entrapped her Father with magic.

She already knew the layout of the inn from her visits there investigating the two homicides. She hadn't known at the time the second death had actually been a suicide. It was remarkable to think the victim had managed to disembowel herself. She had foolishly separated the dagger from its case. The dagger came awake.

And the dagger always demands blood.

The victim inflicted the punishment upon herself, directed by the power of her Father. And given unnatural strength to perform the act.

Lies and blood are alike. They are essential, and they flow like water.

San Marcos had so little crime that it was a boring beat for a detective. Small inns like this one didn't lock their front doors during business hours, even when no one was at the front desk.

Lepore strolled into the Esperanza Inn, the dagger case inside her large handbag. No one was around. She listened. Water ran in the kitchen sink down the hall. That was the only sound.

She climbed the stairs. The second-floor landing was surrounded by a hallway in a square. At each corner was the door to a guest room. A short hallway led to a fifth guest room. The door on the northeast corner was open. Lepore cautiously approached it.

The bed had been stripped of sheets, and the bath was missing its towels. The housekeeper would return to this room soon.

Lepore climbed the stairs to the third floor, listening carefully, but hearing no one. She slowed as her head reached the level of the landing. She surveyed the floor for signs of a cleaning cart, but it wasn't here. On this floor, two rooms were open and stripped of their dirty linens. Not much turnaround in this establishment.

Now, all she had to do was set up an ambush and wait. Should she wait by the elevator for the cart to return? No, guests might be on the elevator.

Instead, she would wait in one of the partly cleaned rooms. When the housekeeper entered it, she would be slain leisurely. Lepore chose the nearest room on this floor to set her trap. She went inside and hid in the closet, which was just past the door. When the housekeeper entered, Lepore would leave the closet, blocking the housekeeper's escape.

She placed her handbag on the floor and withdrew the dagger case. She held it against her chest. It was warm and pulsed in the same rhythm as her heartbeat.

CHAPTER 25

IT MUST TASTE BLOOD

I was cleaning up after breakfast when bells above the front door tinkled. They were tiny bells, but today, they sounded like the church bell of fate. I wiped my hands and went into the foyer. Samson stood there with a uniformed officer.

"Where can we find Ms. Whistler?" Samson asked.

I had, only moments ago, heard the squeaking wheels of the housekeeping cart passing through the service corridor.

"I believe she's in the laundry room," I said. "I'll show you the way."

I led them down the hallway, behind the kitchen, past the storage rooms, and into the former garage.

"Remember, she knows black magic," I whispered to Samson. "Be careful."

"As long as she's not armed, I think we'll be okay," he said sarcastically.

Not long ago, I watched my witch cousin battle a black-magic sorceress. I learned that magic can be more dangerous than firearms. Between the two of them, they probably could have taken on an Army battalion. But magic comes in many forms for a wide variety of uses. Knowing how to summon demons didn't mean you also learned the ability to shoot fireballs from your fingers. I hoped that was the case with Whistler.

She was standing in the outside doorway, smoking a cigarette, when Samson entered the room, flashing his badge, the uniformed officer right behind him.

"Jane Whistler, we have a warrant for your arrest," he said, walking right up to her and seizing her wrists. He recited her Miranda rights as he handcuffed her arms behind her.

She didn't even resist, her eyes wide in astonishment, the cigarette still smoldering between her lips. I expected lightning bolts to shoot from her. Instead, tears rolled down her cheeks.

She had directed three different people to kill me, but I still felt sorry for her. Maybe, because she'd been abandoned by the person she'd dedicated her life to. Maybe because, like me, she was middle-aged, but, unlike me, had no optimistic path forward.

She caught my eyes as she was led out the back door. I expected to see hatred, but all there was in those eyes was a plea for sympathy. That was the only emotion I had left for her.

After everyone had left, I felt emptiness, too. The staff at the Esperanza Inn was so minuscule that losing the woman, formerly known as Julie, made me feel very alone. I called Bella and asked her to work additional shifts and to let me know if she knew of anyone who wanted a housekeeper job.

I returned to the kitchen and washed the baking dishes that had held my egg casserole.

I really needed an assistant, I realized, someone who could fill in wherever they were needed.

Sophie came to mind. That would be an easy choice to make. But I had always dreamed of her becoming the CEO of a large company, or a daring entrepreneur. Not helping out at her mom's business. I suppose the sentimental idea of a family business evaporated when Cory disappeared on me, and I had to run the B & B on my own before selling it. When I opened the Esperanza Inn, I saw it as my business, single-handedly run by the team of me, myself, and I. It was about proving I could do it, that I was strong and independent. It was a far cry from a family business.

Then again, Sophie wasn't having much success on the career front. It would be nice to have someone I could trust and depend on. Someone who wouldn't hire people to kill me.

After I was done in the kitchen, I returned to the scene of the arrest and loaded the cart with fresh towels, sheets, toilet paper, cute French soaps, and little shampoo bottles. I placed my phone on a tray of the cart in front of the handle. And I rolled the cart through the back hallway to the elevator.

I had four rooms to turn around, whose guests had checked out, and two rooms of current guests in which to make beds and tidy up. My now-in-custody housekeeper had already cleaned the four rooms. I only needed to put fresh sheets on the beds and hang towels. I started on the third floor and would work my way down.

The elevator reached the third floor. I rolled the cart into the hallway. Each floor had four rooms arrayed around the landing, some of which I called "suites," and one smaller room in a hall that extended to the east. This was where the elevator was. I rolled the cart to the main landing. Which of the two open rooms should I begin with?

I picked 304.

When I walked in, it felt as if someone was still there. As far as I knew, this room wasn't haunted. I figured I was sensing the psychic energy of former guests clinging to the surfaces they had touched. That showed how strong my psychometry was. The energy was detectable to me, although I hadn't even touched anything yet.

I put on a pair of heavy rubber gloves. I wasn't in the mood to read anyone's memories today.

I passed the closet, and thought about checking it for items left behind, but I had a pile of towels in my arms. I hung them in the bathroom, and placed new soaps, shampoos, and other niceties beside the sink. Then I grabbed sheets and made the bed. It was a sturdy oak four-poster that I adored. It looked like the room had been vacuumed. I ran a cloth across the dark wood surfaces of the furniture. The heavy varnish, meant to be water-ring resistant, had been showing a little dust. Now it gleamed in the late-morning light. I tidied up some more, then left the room, locking it behind me.

Now on to 303. The guest who had checked out had been the first to stay there since the Simpsons. I had received no complaints, so I assumed no evil energy had remained, and the ghost had behaved.

I entered with the towels and bathroom supplies.

As I hung towels, I again sensed psychic energy. But this time, it made my skin tingle and my stomach clench. The energy must be strong for me to feel it so distinctly. Even though I had gloves on to shield myself, I could tell the energy wasn't coming from the towel rods.

There was something familiar about this feeling. It reminded me of the dagger case. Was it possible the energy had remained in the dresser drawer where Simpson had hidden the case?

When I finished in the bathroom, I walked into the bedroom and slowly approached the dresser. Funny, but the energy actually felt weaker over here.

The closet door burst open.

Lepore stepped out, brandishing the dagger.

Oh, *that's* where the energy was coming from.

Lepore closed the door to the room and locked the deadbolt.

And my cellphone was sitting on the cart in the hall.

"You must die to free Father from your magic treachery," she said.

Yeah, I was terrified. But what also freaked me out was the vacant look in Lepore's eyes. She didn't recognize me. She wasn't in there. It was Lepore's face, animated by another being.

And Lepore's hand was holding the dagger, pointing it at my heart.

"You've got the wrong person, Detective Lepore," I said, pretending to be calm. "The person who summoned your father is Jane Whistler. Your partner, Detective Samson, just arrested her."

I don't think she heard a word I said. She moved toward me, crouching slightly, ready to spring if I tried to run past her. She held the dagger like a sword, and to my eyes it looked as long as a sword.

"I'm Darla Chesswick. I own this inn. Don't you remember me?"

"Don't lie to me." Her voice was flat and inhuman. "I am the daughter of the Father of Lies. I know what is true or false."

You're possessed by a demon, I wanted to say, but didn't know if it was a wise thing to say to someone possessed by a demon.

She advanced closer. She was at the end of the bed; I was past it, at the dresser, near the window.

I couldn't jump from the window. I'd seen how that would work out.

I glanced around for a weapon. There wasn't anything in reach except for a floor lamp. I picked it up and held it like a pike, except, instead of a deadly point, it ended with a frilly lampshade and an LED bulb.

"Detective Lepore!" I shouted. "Do you hear me? You are Detective Cynthia Lepore."

She hesitated, blinked her eyes. Her face contorted with an internal struggle.

"Come on, Lepore, snap out of it. How about if I call you Leper? Doesn't that make you angry? Hey! I know you're in there."

Confusion filled her face.

"Drop the dagger and move far away from it," I pleaded. "You'll come back to your senses."

Her eyes looked at me with clarity. But they still weren't Lepore's.

"The dagger must taste blood," Lepore said. She had lost her battle to snap out of it.

"But not my blood. I'm not the person you want. I'm Darla Chesswick. The woman with the black magic has been arrested."

"You're going to die now. The dagger has been removed from its case. And it must taste blood."

"Help!" I screamed. "Help! I'm in three-oh-three! There's another housekeeper here," I said to Lepore. "She's calling the police."

The creature standing in front of me didn't even hear me. And there was no one in the inn to hear me, aside from a gargoyle who remained attached to walls.

She lunged at me. I thrust the lamp at her, hitting her squarely in the chest, keeping myself just out of reach of the dagger.

But she was too strong. She pushed toward me, slashing with the dagger. The frilly lampshade was sliced into pieces.

She grabbed the lamp with her free hand and yanked it from my grasp as easily as if I were a child. She tossed it to the floor.

The dagger gleamed. I knew I was going to die.

I backed toward the window. I really, really did not want to jump, but I was about to.

First, I tried to run past Lepore. A burning sensation crossed my right arm below the shoulder, as Lepore slashed me and blocked my route.

I cowered behind the reading chair. The sleeve of my blouse was drenched in blood.

Now, I was far from the window. I lifted the chair to use it as a shield, but it was heavy, and my right arm was growing numb.

She lunged, and I blocked her with the chair. The dagger passed through the chair's back and almost into me.

She tugged the dagger free, and pulled the chair away from me with only one hand.

"Help," I cried weakly.

I was done.

Something moved behind Lepore. The heavy woolen bedspread, folded at the foot of the sheet-less bed, rose into the air.

Lepore saw my gaze and turned her head to see what was behind her.

The bedspread unfolded and continued to levitate, touching the ceiling with one end.

And then dropped upon Lepore like a net. It drew tightly around her, binding her arms. She couldn't see or move.

So I punched her in the head with my non-bleeding arm as hard as I could. Next, I slammed into her like an NFL lineman and managed to push her backwards, while she struggled to free herself from the bedspread.

I pushed harder, and she went down.

The lamp on the table in the sitting area was heavy brass. I slammed it on the blanketed head of Lepore.

She stopped moving.

Out of the corner of my eye, a woman in a white, floor-length gown with a high collar moved through the room. When I looked in her direction, I saw nothing.

The ghost of 303 had saved me.

I FOUND MY PHONE ON THE CART AND CALLED 911. Immediately afterwards, I called Samson. It went to voicemail.

"I found Detective Lepore," I said.

Even though a cop was supposed to be parked near the inn to look after me, the paramedics arrived at the same time the police did.

The female one cleaned and bandaged my arm, but said I needed to go to the ER for stitches. Fortunately, no major blood vessel had been severed.

I sat on the chair that the dagger had impaled and watched the paramedics work on Lepore. I had grown to respect her. But I have to admit, I returned to disliking her after she tried to kill me.

I know, I know, I'm being too judgmental. Even people who try to kill us can have their good points.

And yes, I realize she was possessed by a demonic force. But still, can't I dislike the woman?

As I watched the paramedics, I hoped she'd be okay. I didn't want to have killed her, especially not with a lamp I bought from Mom's antique store. I wouldn't be able to live with the guilt (for her death, not the lamp).

The paramedics prepared to lift her onto a gurney. Suddenly, her hand shot out and grabbed the dagger from the floor.

Why hadn't the cop moved that out of the way? Because the crime scene techs weren't here yet.

Lepore's eyes fluttered open.

"The dagger must taste blood," she said in the same flat voice.

She lifted the dagger and aimed it at her chest.

"Stop her!" I shouted. "She's going to kill herself."

The three first responders leaped at her and grabbed her arm. As unnaturally strong as she'd been, the three wrestled the dagger from her before she plunged it into her chest.

During the confusion, I grabbed the dagger case I saw on the floor of the open closet. Actually, the dagger *had* tasted blood. Mine. I hadn't died, but I wasn't the one who the demon meant to kill. I hoped the evil weapon would not return to its case ever again.

I threw the case as far as I could out into the hallway.

"Make sure the dagger stays separated from that case in the evidence room," I told the cop. "I'm serious."

Watching Lepore lifted and placed on the gurney, I thought, boy, Samson really owes me now for saving his girlfriend.

CHAPTER 26

LIP BALM

The bells tinkled above the front door, and I tensed. Even with Whistler arrested, I couldn't be certain another assassin wasn't entering my inn. To say I was traumatized by recent events was putting it mildly. I left the kitchen to see who it was.

Samson waited in the foyer. He smirked and looked at my hand.

"I hope you know how to use that," he said.

I looked down at my hand. I hadn't realized I was still holding the chopping knife.

"I know how to use it on onions. So far, not on people. But that could change the way things are going lately. How's Detective Lepore?"

"She's still in the hospital, under psychiatric observation. As far as your blow to her noggin, she only had a mild concussion. As far as being possessed by a demon, well, she didn't accept my explanation for that. Nor did the psychiatrist. She's going to have to undergo thousands of tests before they clear her. As long as the dagger is far away, she should be fine. Hopefully, she can return to duty before long with a clear record."

I didn't wish her ill, but I wouldn't root for her career success, either.

"I'm happy for you that she's all right," I said.

"You're saying it like she's my wife or something."

"Well, your girlfriend."

"What?" He laughed.

"I saw you on a date with her that night at The Wharf restaurant. Don't deny it was a date. You even referred to her as your date when we bumped into each other."

He smiled wryly. "We had a few dates. But soon afterwards, we were assigned to be partners. That put a quick end to any hope for romance."

I tried to hide my pleasure in hearing that.

"Anyway, I'm happy you both survived that horrible experience," he said.

"We'll have challenges getting over it."

"I understand. I can direct you to a crisis counselor."

"Not yet, thanks."

"Let me know if I can help you in any way."

I liked the sound of that much better.

"Oh, I wanted to give you some news," he said. "Because you and I were suspicious of Mewling's death, I asked the medical examiner to do some extra tests during and after the autopsy. Turns out there were large amounts of potassium in his tissue. It's not unusual for a heart attack to cause elevated levels of potassium. But these were excessively high, and the M.E. found a recent syringe puncture between the toes and other suspicious signs. She thinks she has enough evidence consistent with a massive potassium chloride injection."

"What does that do?"

"It causes heart arrhythmias and mimics a heart attack. It's a good way to murder someone without getting caught. But this time, she got caught. The prosecutor is seeing if we can add that to the charges against Whistler."

"Good," I said. "I knew she killed him. Now what about his followers?"

"They'll still be fanatics, for sure. But without Whistler's specific commands to go after you guys, and her black magic to compel them, you should be safe. Remember, Mewling never ranted against you guys by name. The only one who knew about you was Whistler."

"Thank you for updating me," I said. "And for believing in all this supernatural craziness."

"Do I need to remind you of what I am?"

"Turning all hairy each full moon doesn't mean you believe in demons and enchanted daggers."

He smiled. "I'm sure there are closed-minded were-wolves out there. But ever since I worked with my first psychic, I realized the potential. A lot of times it didn't bear fruit, but I've had so many cold cases that could only be solved once I opened my mind to supernatural explanations."

"And how were they prosecuted?"

He laughed. "Few were, but at least, I had the personal satisfaction of solving the crimes."

"Again, thank you."

"You seem eager to get rid of me."

"I have a lot of work to do," I said truthfully. "And, no offense, I've had my fill of law enforcement officers crowding my inn."

"You're a strong woman, Darla," Samson said, trying to catch my eyes, forcing me to not look away. "I want to be sure you're not hurting inside. It's okay to admit you need some help. And I'm offering to lend you my ears."

I could tell he was sincere. And I appreciated his concern. It's good to know a nice-looking guy like him wasn't completely shallow. And, heck, it was good to know someone cared about me. Other than my daughter and mother, who were too caught up in their own lives to put much effort into it.

"Thank you for being so sweet," I said. "Someday I'll take up your offer to listen. But I warn you, I'm a bit bipolar. And when I need to talk, I *need* to talk. You'd have to free up your calendar to hear it all."

"I'm willing to do that," he said softly.

He grasped my shoulders, leaned down, and gave me a kiss on the cheek. An innocent, no-questions-asked peck right below my left cheekbone. Nothing more than a brother would give.

But, I tell you, my cheek tingled like it would never stop.

"Can a non-guest stop by sometime for tea?" he asked as he released my shoulders and headed for the door.

"Absolutely. Just don't eat up all my scones."

AFTER SAMSON LEFT, I TRUDGED UP THE STAIRS TO THE THIRD floor. I needed to inspect 303 and see how much damage had been done. I gasped when I saw the scene for the first time since I almost died.

Paper and plastic wrappings from gauze pads and other medical supplies littered the floor. The bedspread remained in a heap on the hardwood floor. I was tempted to kick it to make sure a psycho killer wasn't beneath it. The brass lamp that bonked Lepore lay beside it, bent at an odd angle, its shade destroyed. The same with the floor lamp I had used to fend off my attacker. Its shade and bulb were gone, and its neck had been warped. The reading chair, an antique like everything else, had a hole in it with stuffing poking out. Lots of things had been knocked out of place, but were okay. The exception was the Persian rug that covered the center of the floor. It was ruined by blood stains. From my blood.

The dagger and case were with the police, of course. Samson promised he would make sure they stayed separated, so the cursed weapon would never kill again or be hijacked by another evil entity.

I ruefully realized we'd done a favor for The Father of Lies. The demon tried to get Dennis and Lepore to kill the woman who had been summoning him. We got her arrested instead. I doubted the demon would show any appreciation for that when the Memory Guild fought against him in the future.

I threw the trash into the basket and removed the plastic bag. I rolled the carpet, careful not to disturb the sutures on my arm. I would bring the carpet somewhere to see if they could remove the stain. Carrying the trash and carpet, I left the room. And stopped.

A trapdoor had appeared on the hallway ceiling. It wasn't in the same place it had been when I fell through it on my return home from the In Between. I wasn't surprised.

I ignored it and went downstairs. But I couldn't get it out of my mind. Nowhere in the inn was one of those poles with hooks on the end that people use to open these attic trapdoors, because the inn didn't have an attic. But I grabbed a rake from the potting shed to improvise.

When I returned to the third floor, I was surprised the trapdoor was still there. Usually, these doors to the nonexistent attic didn't stick around long. The rake successfully grabbed the eyebolt on the door and pulled it open. Ancient springs squealed as the door, with the folded wooden ladder inside, lowered from the ceiling.

I jumped aside as two objects fell out and landed on the carpet runner beside me. The heaviest object was a pistol. Something smaller and lighter bounced and rolled to the wall.

The pistol was compact and black. It wasn't the gun that Sam Spade had when he chased me. Where did it come from?

Then, I remembered. One of Monique Simpson's memories was the aftermath of her husband's death, when she hid the gun in case the police searched her room. She placed it on what she thought was the stairs to the attic. It was actually the gateway to the In Between. And it had disappeared by the time she wanted to retrieve her gun.

Did the gun simply fall from the In Between by chance, or did it come here for a reason? And what was I supposed to do with it? My dad, before he died when I was in high school, took me to the shooting range twice. I simply wasn't that interested in firearms. I wanted to be an artist, and being a chick with a gun didn't fit my image of myself. Though, to be clear, here in North Florida, there are a lot of chicks with guns. My first husband, Buddy, had a gun and I never touched it. And Cory wasn't into guns. I couldn't remember how to clean and maintain them.

Taking some facial tissues from 303, I picked it up to avoid getting my prints on it. Monique hadn't used it to kill her husband, but she planned to use it on me. She might have used it on others. I should give it to the police, I supposed.

The gun was small and not too heavy. Suitable for a petite woman like me. I could ask Samson to run a check on it to see if it had been stolen, or if there were open cases involving shootings with a pistol of this caliber—whatever caliber it was. If not, maybe I would keep it. Lacking tools of self-defense was a big problem for me lately.

I searched for the other object that had fallen from the In Between. It lay against the molding along the floor behind me: a black stick of lip balm with a white top. It seemed familiar, but probably because it was a popular brand. I placed it in my pocket before bringing the gun downstairs and storing it in the inn's safe.

Later that night, before I went to bed, I realized the lip balm was still in my pocket. I placed it on top of my dresser. And stared at it. Its wrap-around label was worn from handling and friction. Removing the cap and twisting the wheel at the end to raise the waxy cylinder showed half of the product remained. When I touched it, I didn't pick up any memories of the owner.

It seemed so familiar. It was just a stupid, inexpensive item. Why would it have any importance to me? I must have a memory buried deep about lip balm.

Too bad I wasn't good at reading my own memories.

Picking it up, I pressed both palms against it and tried to read it again. It simply lacked enough psychic energy for me to read any memories.

But soon, a hazy image came into my mind. I don't think it was from someone else. It was my own mental image.

Of the lip balm sitting atop a dresser next to a comb, handkerchief, loose change, and a wallet.

The items Cory carried in his pockets every day and left on the dresser when he went to bed. And I was certain this was the brand of lip balm that he preferred.

I removed the cap again and touched the tip of the balm—

—and I was Cory, in his sixteen-foot skiff, fishing just off Key West, lips cracked from sun and salt, applying the balm, lips smiling at the sight of a rod tip twitching with a bite—

—I almost collapsed. This was the closest I'd been to Cory since the night he disappeared. My pulse raced. I felt such an intimate connection with him now, though he was as inaccessible to me as ever.

If he was still in the In Between, had he sent me this lip balm as a message?

With my cheek still seeming to tingle from Samson's kiss, I raised the lip balm to my mouth and ran it across my lips.

And luxuriated in the image of Cory's face in my mind, in the memory of the love we'd had.

Much later, when I woke up in the middle of the night, I wondered if he needed my help. Did I have the courage to return to the In Between to look for him? But if I did, how could I find him?

And why was I continuing to flirt with Samson? Once again, I made my life much too complicated.

CHAPTER 27

THE BEACH TROLL

I wondered how Sophie and Imelda met the troll. Supernatural and folkloric creatures don't reveal themselves to just any human, only those with paranormal or magical blood. In fact, the troll and her children would be invisible to normal humans.

I pointed this out to Sophie when I arrived at the state park beach.

She said, "Imelda is from what you could call the Mayan version of the Fae."

"I have the blood of the Aluxes in me."

"Very cool," I said, not knowing what the Aluxes were. I turned to Sophie and looked her up and down questioningly. "And you?"

"It's true, Mom. Grammers always said she thought I had some witch blood in me. Every year, I've felt a stronger pull to learn magic. I think that's why Imelda and I became instant friends. We both sensed the supernatural in each other. I would have told you sooner, but you always wanted so much for me to have a normal life."

I did indeed. But I shouldn't be surprised that Sophie inherited witchy genes. The Chesswick women have had them since my great-grandmother, but probably also before her.

It is possible to have a normal life when you have magic genes. My mother runs an antique business and treats magic more like a hobby. Her sister, on the other hand, turned to evil and is a black-magic sorceress. Then there's me, with my "paranormal" gifts, trying to live a normal life and not quite succeeding.

"Regardless of how much you decide to follow magic," I said to Sophie, "I still want you to build a good career and raise a family."

I wasn't ready yet to decide if she should work for me at the inn.

Sophie rolled her eyes. "Of course, Mom. I would never be a witch for hire like my great-aunt."

"Let's hope not. She's evil and criminal."

"Are you ready to meet Gerta now?" Imelda asked. "We shouldn't keep her waiting."

"I'm ready."

My world had been knocked so far out of whack, that one more freaky experience couldn't hurt.

"Follow us," Sophie said.

I went down the steps to the beach, did a 180, and climbed the dune beside the boardwalk, being careful not to damage the sea oats waving slightly in the breeze. I dragged a cooler on wheels that was filled with the venison Sam Spade left in the inn's refrigerator. We didn't know if beach trolls eat venison, but it seemed like it would be a nice gift.

I followed Sophie and Imelda down the back slope of the

dune. We turned and went beneath the boardwalk where the vegetation was sparser, and the darkness was bisected by regular lines of light seeping down between the boards above.

The two women faced the back of the dune.

"Gerta, we have returned to your doorstep and ask again for your welcome. We have brought my mother to meet you."

We stood in silence for a while, staring at the hill of sand with its few patches of weeds. It was completely unremarkable. There was no indication anyone would live in there.

Then, in the shadows, a greater shade of darkness formed a patch near the bottom of the dune. It grew before our eyes until it resembled the shape of a door with a rounded top. The darkness gained mass, becoming a solid black door.

It opened outward, releasing faint but warm light. Two adorable troll children stood in the opening, male and female of close ages wearing brown onesies of an unknown fabric.

When I said adorable, you must understand the young trolls were bigger than me. Yes, I'm petite, but they were clearly quite young, with the cherub-like faces of human toddlers. The differences were their large, broad noses, bulging foreheads, and pointed ears. They also looked strong enough to play for the University of Florida's football team.

"Hello again, Kristof and Annika," Sophie said. "This is my mother, Darla."

I smiled and waved, too awestruck to say anything.

"Come see Mama," the boy troll said in a squeaky voice that belied his size and strength.

He led us into a small, domed space within the dune, walls and ceiling supported by wooden timbers, that looked old enough to have come from shipwrecks centuries ago. The space was lit by a kerosene lamp hanging from a beam.

To our right, a steep tunnel descended into a cave in the

coquina limestone prevalent in this area's beaches and below ground. We followed it into a space larger than the first one. Candles burned in sconces carved into the coarse, pitted limestone walls. Three cots were arrayed around the perimeter. In the largest one, a full-sized adult beach troll sat in a brown linen night shirt. Her features were like her children's although more pronounced and more weathered and knobbier. She smiled at us.

"Gerta, this is my mother, Darla," Sophie said.

"Pleased to meet you," I said.

"Welcome," the troll said. Her voice was deep and rumbling, like you'd expect of a troll. "I thank you all for the gifts of food for my family while I try to recover from my illness."

"What is it that ails you?" I asked.

"I know not. It has sapped my strength and made it difficult to breathe."

"Are you getting better?"

She didn't answer at first, looked at each of us and her children, before she nodded slowly.

It was a very unconvincing nod.

"My cousin is a witch who has magic that can heal the illnesses creatures, such as you, can get. She's also a nurse. I'll make no promises, but if you allow her to see you, she might be able to help. She should be in San Marcos soon."

"Yes. Please."

"You still want me to visit," Missy asked over the phone, "even after you solved your black magic problems on your own?"

"Yes. I need your magic for healing, not fighting."

I explained the beach troll's illness.

"Hmm, I don't know what she has," Missy said. "I have only two troll patients, both bridge trolls, so I can hardly call myself an expert in their care. But I have some general healing spells that work well on supernaturals. They're worth a try. I don't have any appointments until tomorrow night, so I'll drive up there right away."

A little over four hours later, Missy pulled into a parking spot by the beach. We hugged and kissed. She hugged Sophie, and I introduced her to Imelda.

"Where's the patient? I'm ready to get to work," Missy said.

"Don't you need to rest after your long drive?" Sophie asked.

"No. I used the quiet time to gather my internal energies, to prime the pump, so to speak. So my magic is ready to flow."

We led her underneath the boardwalk to the spot where the troll den was hidden. After we requested entrance, the door appeared, and the two troll children opened it for us.

When Missy met Gerta, she said, "Oh, my. Beach trolls are even prettier than bridge trolls."

Gerta smiled, though she appeared weaker than when we last saw her.

Missy opened her tote bag and did what I wasn't expecting: a cursory medical examination of the troll. It was just like the kind we humans get, complete with stethoscope, thermometer, oxygen finger clip, and blood-pressure cuff.

Missy frowned at the results she was seeing.

"Do you have any reason to suspect a witch or wizard has hexed you?" she asked.

Gerta shook her head no.

"Let me make sure there's no malignant magic in you."

Missy took a cloth amulet from her bag and pressed it against Gerta's head and several places on her body.

"Nope. No black magic," she said. "I can't identify your

specific illness. It may be unique to trolls. But I will try some spells that have broad healing capabilities. Please lie back and get comfortable."

It must have been two hours that Missy spent in that limestone cave. She knelt within a magic circle she scratched on the sand floor, intoning verses in strange languages. She sprinkled unidentified herbs on her patient's head and had her drink a vial's worth of an amber potion that made Gerta grimace from its taste. Then she returned to her magic circle.

I thought the entire effort was going to be a bust, but then I noticed something: a greenish glow surrounded Gerta's head, and her eyes closed.

Missy watched her with anticipation for what seemed like an eternity.

The glow faded. But Gerta's face was no longer pale like before. It looked healthy and ruddy.

The troll's eyes popped open. Her face lit up with a big, toothy smile.

"I feel wonderful!"

Missy sighed with relief. "Excellent. Now, you'll want to rest for a few days while you . . ."

Gerta leaped out of her cot. We're talking a seven-foot-tall creature weighing at least 300 pounds springing out of bed like a cat.

She danced a jig in the middle of the floor, her two children jumping up and down with delight.

". . . get your strength back," Missy said.

"Thank you for curing me," Gerta said, picking Missy up with one hand and squeezing her against her chest.

I tried to get out of the way, but she grabbed me and did the same, followed by Sophie and Imelda. There were too many bodies celebrating in that cave, so eventually, we humans said our goodbyes and took our leave.

We took Missy out to dinner to celebrate at a favorite water-front Cuban restaurant. Halfway through the meal, Sophie shared some news.

"Billy came by to visit Grammers today," she said.

"He's as dependable as the sun rising in the east."

"He mentioned the detective who attacked you—what's her name, Lepore?"

"Leper. Detective Leper."

"He said she's been sent to a mental-health facility. And she probably won't have a job when she gets out. At least not as a detective."

"Really?"

"Yeah," Sophie said. "Billy said the department is taking her unprovoked attack on a civilian very seriously. And that she used an unauthorized weapon. Even if she's completely cleared for mental health, they wouldn't trust her again."

Samson knew she wasn't mentally ill; she'd been possessed by a demon. But how could he tell that to the department brass? Telling them wouldn't help Lepore at all, and it would harm his career.

"I'm sad for her," I said. "But she tried to kill me. Anyway, on a lighter note, do you think Grammers is slipping a love potion into the scones she feeds Billy?"

Sophie nodded. "I accidentally put a leftover scone from the first batch in with the second batch she bakes for the customers. A twelve-year-old boy ate it, then told me he was madly in love with me. He found a used book by Elizabeth Barrett Browning upstairs, and read all of her love sonnets aloud to me. Every single one. There's more than forty of them! Thank God his mother took him away."

"Oh, no. She probably used a potion targeted to younger men, because Billy is younger."

"I'll tell her she needs to make big adjustments," Sophie said.

AFTER DESSERT, WHEN THE TWO YOUNGER WOMEN WERE immersed in a conversation of their own, I spoke to Missy in a voice low enough to not be overheard.

"I went to the In Between," I said.

"Oh, my. I told you not to do that."

"I had no choice, I was trying to escape from a killer with a gun, and when the gateway appeared, it was my only chance."

"Oh." She couldn't argue with that. "How did you get back home?"

"Dragons showed me where to find some humans who live there, and they brought me to a gateway."

"Humans live there? *Living* humans?"

"Yes. There are a few. They sustain themselves with food and water created with magic. But they can't stay there full time. They have to return to our dimension from time to time to sort of reconstitute their molecular structure, or something like that."

I leaned closer to Missy and whispered, "One of them said she had seen Cory there."

Missy's eyes opened wide. "Really?"

"Yes. There was something about him seeking a wizard who lived there to help him develop powers he had discovered within himself."

"This is too strange. What do you think about it?"

"I want to find him somehow. I wonder, though, why he

hasn't returned to me after all this time, knowing now that he would have the ability to return. Unless he didn't survive. Or was captured by someone. Or something."

"Don't go back there looking for him. It's too dangerous. You wouldn't know where to begin. And the gateways can dump you in random spots all over the place. You might not be able to get back here again."

"I know. I'm not going to do anything for now. I'll wait until I think of a plan. Or receive a sign of some kind."

"Let me know before you do anything," Missy said. "You shouldn't go alone."

But for the past year, I've been able to muddle through life alone. Somehow.

OUTSIDE THE RESTAURANT, BEFORE WE WENT OUR SEPARATE ways, the four of us stood on the pier and stared at the water. It glowed with reflections of the lights on the marina docks and from the city street lamps along the waterfront. Now and then, small fish made "*plip*" sounds at the water's surface.

I led Sophie aside.

"I'm sorry I was suspicious of you," I said. "You mean the world to me, and I guess I'm overprotective while pretending that I'm not."

She smiled warmly, the running light from a sailboat reflected in her eyes.

"I understand, Mom. I've put you through a lot over the years. And I've taken a lot of money from you. Someday, I hope to pay you back."

"You'll pay me back by living a full and happy life."

"Someday, I'll take care of you."

"I won't be a decrepit old lady," I said. "I'll be independent to the end."

"I'll still take care of you in one way or another."

"You need to take care of yourself first," I said. "You have a lot on your shoulders. Staying sober is a lot of work. And now, it's confirmed that you have the paranormal genes of the Chesswick women."

"You say it like it's a negative thing."

"It's a gift, but it can become a negative force if you let it. If you use it like a crutch to make things easier for you. Or if you're tempted to misuse it for evil like your great-aunt."

"I told you I would never do that. I'm not even sure what kind of power I have."

"It's not power," I said sternly. "It's ability. There's a difference. You need to understand that."

"How do I learn more?"

"Grammers and I will work with you and help you see what you've got. Then help you develop it responsibly. After that, you might want to train with an expert. But remember, it could take years for your abilities to emerge."

"Like you?"

"Exactly."

"Then I have plenty of time."

I laughed and hugged her as we walked back to the others.

"The time will go by a heck of a lot faster than you think."

THE NEXT MORNING, I MADE A SPECIAL BREAKFAST FOR MISSY and all the guests at the inn. Belgian waffles with raspberry syrup, eggs Benedict, Southern grits, and avocado toast. Then Missy went on her way back to Jellyfish Beach.

And I turned my attention to fixing the wreckage Whistler left behind. The good news was the things that truly mattered to me were too strong to need fixing.

WHAT'S NEXT

GET A FREE E-BOOK

Sign up for my newsletter and get *Hangry as Hell*, a humorous paranormal novella, for free. Find out more about Darla's cousin, Missy, and her crazy life wrangling retired vampires, werewolves, and other monsters. You'll be the first to know about my new releases and lots of free book promotions. The newsletter is delivered only a couple of times a month. No spam at all, and you can unsubscribe at any time. Sign up to get your free book at wardparker.com.

ENJOYED THIS BOOK? PLEASE LEAVE A REVIEW

The number of reviews readers leave can make or break a book. I would be very grateful if you could spend just a few minutes and write a fair and honest review on the website of the retailer that sold you this book. It can be as short or long as you wish. Thank you so much!

NEXT IN THE MEMORY GUILD MYSTERIES:

A WICKED TOUCH

Keep your hands to yourself.

There I go again, touching things I shouldn't.

A knife my antique-dealer mother bought at an estate sale holds the memories of a terrified young woman about to be abducted by a werewolf.

You see, I'm a psychometrist. I can read the memories people leave behind on the objects they touch. And this ability gets me into a lot of trouble.

I feel obligated to save the young woman before she is killed. And it turns out that she's not the first woman this shifter has taken. Nor will she be the last. The others are turning up dead.

I'm a member of the supernatural Memory Guild, but I'm no detective. (I do, however, have a sexy detective helping me.) I'm just a middle-aged innkeeper with a 300-year-old bed-and-breakfast, a witchy mother, and a trouble-prone daughter. All of them demand a lot of attention.

When you throw into the mix an evil necromancer raising the dead, and an ancient magical stone, well, things get wicked complicated.

And I have to solve this mystery before someone else is killed. Namely me.

Enjoy midlife mystery, magic, murder, and mischief, with ties to the Freaky Florida humorous paranormal series.

Get *A Wicked Touch* at wardparker.com

HAVE YOU READ FREAKY FLORIDA?

Check out this series of humorous paranormal mysteries featuring Darla's cousin, Missy.

Centuries-old vampires who play pickleball. Aging were-wolves who surf naked beneath the full moon. Plus dragons, demons, ghouls, and more. They're all in Florida, land of the weird, where even monsters come to retire. That's how Missy Mindle comes in. She's started over in midlife as a home health nurse for elderly monsters and as a witch with growing powers. She uses her magick to solve mysteries, with a little help from a cute reporter. But dangerous secrets from the parents she never knew keep bubbling up.

You can start with a free novella when you sign up for my newsletter at wardparker.com

Or, dive right into Book 1, *Snowbirds of Prey*. Find it at ward-parker.com

ABOUT THE AUTHOR

Ward is a Florida native and author of the Freaky Florida series, a romp through the Sunshine State with witches, vampires, werewolves, dragons, and other bizarre, mythical creatures such as #FloridaMan. His newest series is the Memory Guild midlife paranormal mysteries. He also pens the Zeke Adams Series of Florida-noir mysteries and The Teratologist Series of historical supernatural thrillers. Connect with him on social media: Twitter (@wardparker), Facebook (wardparkerauthor), BookBub, Goodreads, or wardparker.com

ALSO BY WARD PARKER

The Zeke Adams Florida-noir mystery series. You can buy *Pariah* and *Fur* at wardparker.com

The Teratologist series of historical paranormal thrillers. Buy the first novel at wardparker.com